CW01278761

'You may have noticed what I am wearing,' Laurie began, smoothing her hips.

Ben's mouth twitched as he calculated his reply. 'Yes,' he said slowly. 'I had noticed. I was too polite to mention it, of course. Is it a new fashion?'

'It's sackcloth and ashes,' said Laurie.

'Ah . . .' he nodded. 'And I thought it was a couple of dustbin liners.'

'I've come to apologise for . . . for my behaviour this morning. I spoke without thinking.'

'Thank you for coming in sackcloth and ashes,' Ben said. 'I appreciate the gesture.'

She struggled to get out of the bin bags and Ben knelt down, hiding his laughter, to help her get divested. 'This is like peeling a ripe banana,' he chuckled, his fingers sliding over her damp skin.

She emerged from the plastic, hot and dishevelled, her trim navy swimsuit dark with perspiration. His eyes relished the soft swell of her bosom and the shadowy cleft that promised such tantalising sweetness. He leaned forward and pushed back her hair, his fingers brushing the lobe of her ear. She caught her breath with a sense of pleasure and turned, without thinking, towards him.

'I think you had better go.'

Stella Whitelaw's writing career began as a cub reporter on a local newspaper. She became one of the first and youngest women Chief Reporters in London. While bringing up her small children she had many short stories published in leading women's magazines. She is deeply interested in alternative medicines and is glad that her son, now a doctor and anaethetist, has an open mind about them. A painful slipped disc has improved since practising the Alexander Technique daily. Her three beautiful long-haired cats inspired her six published cat books.

To the Fellside School of Alexander Technique and the Society of Teachers of the Alexander Technique, with many thanks for their kindness and guidance.

BAPTISM OF FIRE

BY

STELLA WHITELAW

MILLS & BOON LIMITED
ETON HOUSE   18-24 PARADISE ROAD
RICHMOND   SURREY   TW9 1SR

All the characters in this book have no existence outside the imagination of the Author, and have no relation whatsoever to anyone bearing the same name or names. They are not even distantly inspired by any individual known or unknown to the Author, and all the incidents are pure invention.

All Rights Reserved. The text of this publication or any part thereof may not be reproduced or transmitted in any form or by any means, electronic or mechanical, including photocopying, recording, storage in an information retrieval system, or otherwise, without the written permission of the publisher.

This book is sold subject to the condition that it shall not, by way of trade or otherwise, be lent, resold, hired out or otherwise circulated without the prior consent of the publisher in any form of binding or cover other than that in which it is published and without a similar condition including this condition being imposed on the subsequent purchaser.

First published in Great Britain 1989
by Mills & Boon Limited

© Stella Whitelaw 1989

Australian copyright 1989
Philippine copyright 1989
This edition 1989

ISBN 0 263 76463 X

Set in Baskerville 10 on 11 pt.
03 – 8906 – 63100

Typeset in Great Britain by JCL Graphics, Bristol

Made and Printed in Great Britain

CHAPTER ONE

As LAURIE checked her route north for the sixth time, fifty miles away a man was cursing his luck for getting a flat on the motorway. Neither knew they were on a collision course that would set sparks flying from one end of Cumbria to the other.

It was beginning to rain. In moments it was pelting against the windscreen, the wipers slicing ineffectually through the water. Laurie slowed down as visibility worsened. She must stop at the next service station for coffee and petrol. It would be her last chance to fill the tank before leaving the motorway for the Lake District.

'Come on, old girl. You can make it,' she urged her eighteen year old Austin Princess. 'Please don't run out of petrol now.' This was not the time to get lost or stranded. Laurie had too much at stake. A tidy slice of her future.

She coasted into an almost deserted car-park. There were a few lorries, trucks, a couple of cars. She filled the tank with petrol first, then put the Austin near the neon-lit entrance, switched off the engine, turned up the collar of her denim blouson jacket and ran through the rain.

It was steamy warm inside; the cafeteria offered bright islands of food and light. Laurie took a tray and could not resist the display of tempting carbohydrates. She selected a jam doughnut to go with a large cup of coffee. Sugar, she thought, that's what she needed, instant energy to keep going. She paid for her refreshments, noting that the Asian girl cashier looked almost as sleepy as she felt. She saw an empty table tucked away in a far corner and made a bee-line for it, though there was

5

hardly any need to hurry, but a nurse was conditioned to move fast.

'Ouch!'

'Sorry,' she said automatically to a burly truck driver into whom she had almost collided. She blinked her soft hazel eyes and pushed her long spiky fringe aside. She was feeling drowsy and the warmth of the place was sending waves of inertia through her. It was an effort to stand.

The truck driver blocked her way. Steely grey eyes glared down at her, aggressive and unforgiving. She knew what he was thinking. With her silky light brown hair tied back in a loose plait, no make-up and wearing denim jeans and top, she looked about sixteen. The man was six foot two, towering above her, powerful shoulders in a black leather jacket, long legs in scuffed and muddied black jeans. His face was like granite, dark hair with grey-flecked sideburns sculpting high cheek bones, strong nose and well-shaped, curving lips. But it was his eyes that were so disconcerting—they were like laser beams.

'Going somewhere?' he asked abruptly.

She knew what he meant. 'I don't hitch-hike,' she said coolly. 'Excuse me, I'd like to drink my coffee before it gets cold.'

'Mine's in the saucer thanks to you,' he said. 'And don't ever hitch-hike. It's dangerous. You look too young to be out on your own at this time of night. Have you run away from home?'

Laurie pushed past the man without answering. She did not want to talk to anyone. And he was far too big and pushy. She wanted to sit somewhere quietly and drink her coffee. Besides she knew enough about encouraging strangers in the middle of the night and was used to being careful.

'How old are you?' he persisted.

'I don't think that's any of your business,' she said.

'Now, if you don't mind . . .'

She hurried away, sliding into the corner seat and sitting down, hands clasped round the hot cup. It was strong and steaming—coffee had never tasted so good. She sank her teeth into the doughnut, grains of sugar clinging to her full lips.

The truck driver sauntered by with his tray. 'You'll rot your teeth,' he said.

She glared at his broad back. He was a pain and she hoped he wasn't going to sit at the same table. But he didn't, finding a table further down the row. She watched him tuck into toast and marmalade. She noticed his strong hands moving from plate to cup. He was a decisive man. She had observed hands for years in nursing. He would drive his giant container lorry fast and sure, with confident skill and precision.

Her thoughts began to stray as she relaxed. She chased specks of sugar round the plate with her finger, making patterns. She felt her eyelids droop and let them close momentarily.

She felt like a pioneer woman setting off across a prairie in a covered wagon. Her entire possessions were packed in the car, cases, cartons, boxes and bags. She was leaving London behind forever.

'A new life, new roots,' she thought for the hundredth time, still trying to convince herself that she was doing the right thing. Everyone at St Ranuph's thought that she was leaving because of Bruce, the young houseman who was sweet on her, but she wasn't. It was far more complicated. Bruce was a friend but not a man to break hearts, not Laurie's heart anyway.

She had left because she was tired of being a waitress, a bedmaker, a bedpan sluicer and since her promotion to junior sister, a paper pusher. She wanted there to be more to nursing than writing endless reports; the pride was being filtered out of the profession. She wanted to heal bodies and minds, not just hand round meal trays and chart temperatures.

'What a waste, Sister Young,' said the Nursing Administrator with a sniff of disapproval. 'The Alexander Technique? Isn't that some fringe thing? I wish you would reconsider your decision to leave. Think of all your training.'

Sixty per cent of which I never use, Laurie had wanted to say. She had stood on the threadbare mat in the office so often. Her sharp tongue had got her into trouble many times.

'I've nothing against orthodox medicine,' Laurie had replied. 'My training will still be useful. But I think there is a desperate need for other medical principles. Treating the body as a whole, for instance, not just the symptoms. I believe I can help people to live fuller and healthier lives.'

'And don't drive if you're too tired,' the trucker said, pausing on his way out. He loomed over the table, big and dark, his eyes glinting. 'Put your head down and sleep for an hour.'

'Thank you very much for nothing,' she snapped awake. 'I happen to be well aware of the danger of driving when tired and that's why I stopped for some coffee. As for sleeping in my car, there isn't room. I don't have a cab with a convenient bunk and sleeping bag.'

'Be my guest,' he drawled.

'No thank you,' she said politely. She was beginning to tire of his unwelcome advice and was getting nervous of his attentions. But outwardly she remained calm. She would have another coffee, splash her face with cold water in the ladies room, and hope the truck driver would be miles away before she returned to the motorway.

'No thank you,' he repeated, using the same inflexion. It turned the phrase almost into an insult. In other circumstances, Laurie would have given him a smart answer, but the empty cafeteria and deserted car-park outside warned her not to be rash.

She got up quickly and brushed past him to fetch another coffee from the hot drinks counter. She was keenly aware of his size and closeness in the narrow aisle. Laurie had an acute sense of smell despite the years of being immersed in an atmosphere of disinfectant. He didn't smell like a truck driver. He smelt of good soap and aftershave, though she supposed long distance truckers were paid well and entitled to buy expensive brands. There was no reason to think that because he behaved like an arrogant bully, all his tastes were on the same level.

When she returned to the same table, he was just pushing open the exit doors. She glimpsed his tall figure going out into the darkness, shoulders hunched against the rain. She noticed the one-sided stiffness in his neck and stooping shoulders. His posture while driving was storing up back problems for him . . .

Laurie sighed. She couldn't correct everyone's bad habits. They had to come to her and they had to want to be helped. She could not force the Alexander Technique on reluctant patients, for the cure in the end came from within the self.

The caffeine in the second cup of coffee invigorated a degree of her normal alertness, and after a quick wash, she felt ready to continue her journey to the Lake District. It was nearly two months since she had been interviewed in London by James Robinson, the head of a recently established School of Alexander Technique near Windermere. It was not a health farm or health club but a residential school where pupils could come for a week or longer and receive a sound basic training in a group on which to develop their technique. Teachers also gave further private lessons, and were able to see non-residential pupils in the afternoons.

'You'll be able to build up your practice with private
pupils at the school,' said James Robinson. 'There's a
tremendous interest in the area, and as you know, the
follow up work is just as important. We also get many
people, from all walks of life, who simply can't spare a
whole week.'

There were three other registered teachers on the
school's staff and he was sure that Laurie, with her
combined nurses' training and experience, would be an
asset. Laurie had already discovered from the school's
printed stationery that James Robinson was a qualified
doctor and on the Register of Practitioners of the British
Homeopathic Association. Laurie was interested in the
theory that 'like cures like' but knew little about it.

'Do you want me to wear a uniform?' Laurie asked,
when he confirmed that she had the job. She expected the
school might be more formal than the classes she had been
attending in London.

'Uniform?' he guffawed with laughter, his grizzled red
beard shaking. 'No uniform and not much pay either!
Just wear whatever is loose and comfortable for moving
about and around your pupil. The pay will be poor, even
by nursing standards, but you'll get most of your keep
and a little flatlet in the turret.'

'In the turret?' The words were magic. Laurie had
lived in a room in the nurses' home for so long, and the
thought of somewhere private and actually her own was
exhilarating.

'We have a flat in the turret. Don't worry, it isn't
haunted even though Cumthwaite Hall was once the
home of Benedictine nuns. The stairs to the turret are too
narrow and steep for guests. And for the same reason, the
furniture in it is fairly limited,' he added, his light blue
eyes twinkling. 'But wait till you see Cumthwaite Hall
itself. The original ancient pile, beautiful Cumbrian stone

and mullion windows. And the view of the lake is magnificent. We've 123 acres of ground, right down to the water's edge. Acres of peace, I call it.'

Acres of peace. His description clinched it for Laurie. It was what she wanted, what her soul needed. Never mind the taunts of her colleagues and the low pay. She had herself to heal if she was ever to be whole again.

James Robinson explained that Cumthwaite Hall could accommodate about twenty pupils a week in double and single rooms, giving a ratio of one teacher to four to five pupils for the personal supervision which was good. There was a lounge and dining-room but the school only provided a self-service buffet breakfast of health foods and fruit. All other meals had to be taken out, though guests were allowed to use a small kitchen for heating drinks.

'It works well. People mostly go out in the afternoons, sightseeing in Bowness or Windermere, or relax in the grounds if they've booked an extra lesson in the afternoon. They seem to prefer not to be tied to a rigid meal structure and we, quite honestly, couldn't afford the residential catering staff. We've a local woman who comes in to do the breakfasts, and cleaners at the weekend for the turn round.'

'It sounds great,' said Laurie, liking the arrangements more and more. 'When can I start?'

'When can you give notice?' he asked.

Now she had burned her boats despite universal disapproval. Anyone would think she was turning to a life of crime, she thought despondently.

Laurie had discovered the technique by accident. A young woman was brought into Casualty one snowy day with a badly cut forearm. She had slipped on the ice putting out her milk bottles. When Laurie had pulled aside the cubicle curtains she had found the woman laying on her back, knees bent, the back of her head supported by a wedge of folded blanket.

'Sorry, Nurse. I hope you don't mind,' she said.
'Couldn't waste the time and I might have hurt my back in
that fall. So I thought a few minutes of semi-supine wouldn't
come amiss.' The woman noticed the blank look on Laurie's
face. 'I'm putting the fluid back in my discs,' she explained.
'I'm a singer and it's important to have a strong back.
Singing is very strenuous, you know.'

Laurie nodded though she did not understand totally.
Semi-supine? It sounded like a low fat yoghurt.

'Anything to make you feel relaxed,' said Laurie
encouragingly as she cleaned the wounds.

'Oh, it's not a relaxation technique, heavens no. It's far
more than that.' The woman was about to launch in to what
was obviously her pet subject, when a doctor arrived to put a
stitch in the worst of the cuts.

As the woman rose to leave, her arm bandaged, Laurie
noticed her beautiful upright posture and her easy effortless
way of moving, almost like a native woman. There was no
stiffness, no hunching, every part of her body balanced and
free.

'What did you say you were doing?' asked Laurie,
helping her into her coat.

'The semi-supine—it's part of the Alexander Technique.
I do it every four or five hours, and especially before I go on
stage. You ought to make it part of your life, nurses are
always hurting their backs, aren't they?'

Laurie had only that week strained her back lifting a
heavy patient, and she had been suffering a nagging pain in
the lumbar region ever since.

'Oh, I haven't time for anything like that,' Laurie said
more cheerfully than she felt. 'We just have to put up with
backache. Take a few pain killers.'

'You should make more time,' said the singer as she left.
Every movement was fluid but controlled. 'You've only got

one back, and one life.'

Laurie never saw the woman again but their brief conversation stayed in her mind. Then came that Saturday night in Casualty. Saturday nights were always busy especially when the pubs closed and the drunks were wheeled in, but this was different . . . a dark, treacherous night following an international football final. Loud voices and running footsteps crowded into her mind, clattering trollies, overturned instrument trays, smashing glass. Harsh and discordant sounds that heralded a nightmare. Even now Laurie began to tremble at the memory and she forced her hands to tighten round the steering wheel to still them. She would not think about it at all, she told herself. She was capable of putting it out of her mind, she was . . . She had to be strong. She had to be a survivor.

'I hope you know what you're doing, Laurie,' said Bruce, confronting her in the noisy and crowded hospital cafeteria. She was trying to force down congealed shepherd's pie and cold sprouts. She hoped he was not going to start lecturing her.

'Oh, I do, Bruce,' she replied with conviction. 'I do indeed. And I'm really looking forward to it.'

Bruce's round smooth face looked worried. Laurie noticed that his fair hair was already thining or perhaps it was just the harsh light. But it was more likely that hospital hours were taking their toll.

'It all sounds a crack-pot idea,' he said. 'You're probably still suffering from concussion or delayed confusion. It can happen. Why don't you ask for leave and think it over more carefully?'

'I have thought it over carefully,' said Laurie. 'For some years. And it's hardly a crack-pot idea when Matthias Alexander began teaching his method in Auckland as long ago as 1894, and there are hundreds of qualified teachers now all over the world. Ninety-nine per cent of the population misuse their body with bad posture and muscular tension and they don't know what to do about it.'

'That's all very well but ninety-nine per cent of the population don't live in the Lake District,' he said wearily. 'Can't you at least do whatever it is in London? Have I said or done something to upset you? Is it my fault? I know we haven't had much time together recently . . .'

'Heavens no, it's nothing to do with you.' Laurie realised immediately as a spasm of hurt crossed his face that the phrase was not well chosen. She really hated hurting Bruce because he was so nice, but he did not listen to a word she said. For months she had been trying to disengage herself from his single-minded insistence that they had something going between them. They didn't and never had. It was all wishful thinking on his part.

She tried to lighten the atmosphere. 'Stop worrying about me. Windermere isn't in the Amazonian rain forest. I shan't be consumed by crocodiles. At least I don't think there are any roaming the lake. It's only a few hours up the motorway, Bruce. You'll be able to visit me . . . often.'

'That isn't the point,' he said, thumping his tray down on the table. 'You're going away and I don't like it.'

Laurie remained patient. She knew it was not easy for him to understand. He saw everything from his own point of view, never hers. Nothing she could say would change the rigidity of his thinking.

The distance already seemed twice as far, thought Laurie as she ran from the exit doors through the rain and unlocked the door to her car. Inside everything smelled wet and damp. She had left a crack of window open and a steady trickle of rain had found its way in.

'Sugar!' she said, rummaging for a towel to dry the steering wheel and something dry to sit on. But at least the discomfort would keep her awake.

The first rays of dawn were lightening the sky as she

drove through the quiet and empty streets of Windermere, the hillside town above the lake. Below, the water was like a sheet of rose and silver, reflections of ancient trees mirrored darkly on its still surface. Laurie would have liked to find somewhere to admire the view but she was so near her destination, it would have to wait.

She followed the directions to Cumthwaite Hall. No one was about, not even an early milkman. She could have been the only person awake, but she knew there were plenty of night workers and insomniacs. The local hospital would be stirring, the night staff starting the early morning duties.

The trees were thick and overhanging in the lane that followed the curve of the lake and lead to Cumthwaite Hall. It was clearly sign-posted so Laurie knew she was going the right way. She could hardly wake up anyone when she reached the hall, she would take a walk down to the lake and wait for the breakfast helper who must arrive early.

She saw the iron gates of the drive loom ahead, massive and imposing. As she slowed down and turned in, she was suddenly blinded by headlights straight into her eyes. Her reaction was instant and automatic. Her feet crashed down into an emergency stop and only her seat-belt saved her from being thrown against the steering wheel. But still all the breath was knocked out of her.

It was a big gleaming metallic car, a wide chrome radiator and long bonnet blocking the drive, its headlights like beacons. Laurie blinked, shielding her eyes from the glare.

'What the hell are you doing here at this time of night?' a voice shouted as the driver's window automatically rolled down. It was a deep and angry male voice.

Laurie took a shuddering breath, gathering her scattered senses, going rapidly over the sequence of events. She was convinced she had not done anything wrong. So why hadn't she seen the big car coming out of the drive?

She had been trained to observe and make conclusions. Suddenly she knew. She sat back carefully, rubbing her chest, relieved that there was no pain in breathing. She was only sore and bruised. She wound down her window. The other driver's face was in darkness but she glimpsed a glint of rimmed spectacles in her own headlights.

'Don't you know its against the law to drive without headlights on?' she said, her voice sweet and lethal. 'Even in a private driveway.' She did not know if this was strictly true but she doubted if the driver would argue the point. He had only switched on his lights as he reached the junction with the lane. She would have seen their beam earlier if they had been on.

'I suppose you've been out to an all night party?' he countered, going straight for the attack. 'Coming home at four in the morning with slow reactions.'

Laurie knew her reaction had been fast so she didn't rise to that one, but she did not care for the snide party remark. It sounded as if he was a man who didn't get invited to many.

'And I suppse you're just off to work,' she said. 'The milk depot, is it? I hope you'll be in better control of your float.'

She heard his suppressed gasp of rage and felt highly pleased with herself.

'Will you get out of my way?' he roared. 'This is an emergency.'

'An emergency? Are you sure you are in a fit state to deal with an emergency? The first requisite, I imagine, is to be cool and calm. You don't sound as if you are being either.'

He flicked his headlights on and off and put his fist hard on the horn.

'Breaking the law again,' she shouted.

'Get out of my way, woman.'

'With pleasure,' she said even more sweetly. 'I'm rather good at reversing and I wouldn't like you to damage those nice trees.'

Laurie took her time, checking everything elaborately, then reversing smoothly out of his way, giving him plenty of room to pass in the lane. Seconds later, a long Mercedes Estate flashed past with only inches to spare. It accelerated fast. She caught a glimpse of the driver's profile, grim and craggy, gold-rimmed spectacles perched on a strong nose. He did not glance once in her direction but sped off towards the main road.

She paused, disquietened. She had seen that face before and recently. Surely there couldn't be two men in this part of England who looked so alike, despite obvious differences. The spectacles and expensive car were those of a professional. The truck driver had worn black leather and jeans and his manner had been roadwise. But their faces were so similar, the same strong jaw, dark hair, grey-flecked sideburns. Even the same deep, brown voice though now the rich timbre had been distorted by anger.

Laurie sat back, shaking her head. She must be more tired than she had thought. Perhaps she was mistaken. She just hoped that the brutish driver was nothing to do with Cumthwaite Hall and the School of Alexander Technique. It would be too much if her new lakeside paradise had a dragon lurking in it. And a bad-tempered one at that.

CHAPTER TWO

'OH MY goodness! You gave me quite a fright! I didn't expect to find anyone sitting on the doorstep like a little elf. Come on in, you look frozen. Have you lost your key?'

'I don't actually have a key yet. But I would like to come in,' said Laurie, unfolding herself from the stone step.

Laurie followed the bustling, roundly-formed woman into a tiled lobby and then through into a big, modern kitchen. Chrome-topped surfaces gleamed in the half-light as the woman hung up her coat, flipped up blinds and plugged in the electric kettle, all in one continuous movement.

'You must be the breakfast lady,' Laurie went on.

'That's right. I'm Olive.'

'I was hoping you would arrive early. I've been sitting in my car but I couldn't sleep. It's a bit cramped. Then I walked down by the lake but the mist was so thick, I stepped into some water.'

'That's easily done. You've got to know the water's edge, especially in the mist. You'll be needing a cup of tea or you'll catch your death. I'll find you a towel. Are you joining a course or are you the new teacher they are expecting?'

'I'm Laurie Young, the new teacher.'

'I thought so. The students don't usually arrive till the evening, seeing the course starts on Monday morning.'

Laurie was amazed at the speed at which Olive worked. Her short, sturdy legs propelled her round the kitchen like

18

lightning. In no time, the tea was made and poured out, Laurie had towels to dry her feet, and Olive was preparing muesli from a vast selection of assembled bags and cartons.

'We could do with you at St Ranulph's,' said Laurie sipping the welcome tea. 'Our catering staff was always slipping into a state of permanent paralysis. Ask for a special diet and they looked at you as if you'd requisitioned green cheese from the moon.'

'I don't believe in standing about when there's plenty to do,' said Olive, piling apples and grapes into the sink to wash and gulping tea at the same time. 'This is a small breakfast seeing how it's only staff this morning; you should see me with my skates on tomorrow morning.'

'Can I help?' Laurie asked as she wandered round in bare feet. She screwed up her wet pop socks, reminding herself to wash them out later.

'That would be nice. Put some water into the Conas to boil for coffee. The grounds are in the tin. Follow the directions on the packet. They like it good and strong here.'

Laurie found two Conas, filled them with water and measured coffee grounds into the filter. The aroma of the Kenya, French and Columbian blend was heady—a far cry from hospital instant brown.

'Perhaps you could help me carry some things through. I lay it all out on the buffet table in the dining-room and they help themselves.'

Laurie followed Olive along another short passage to tall double doors which she heaved open with a shoulder.

Laurie drew in a breath of admiration. It was a beautifully proportioned room, with long windows, draped with pale green silk curtains, that looked distantly towards the lake. It had a fine corniced ceiling with ornate plasterwork of scrolls and flowers. A handsome stone fireplace dominated the far end of the room, its wide mantle displaying china vases and ornaments that looked old and valuable. A collection of Lakeland paintings hung on the panelled walls, adding lightness and giving the impression of tranquil scenery inside as well as outside the hall.

'What a lovely room,' said Laurie, stopping to admire a big painting of the high, undulating Skiddaw. She strolled along—Windermere, Ullswater, Eagle Crag, Borrowdale, Langdale Pass—each painting was mysterious and emotive, something of the ancient history of the Cumbrian landscape caught in the swirling mist and shimmering sun.

'Isn't it? Nothing's been changed. This is the same big table as used by the family. It's hundreds of years old. We brought in some small tables for the guests to sit at, but there were plenty around the house.'

Laurie vaguely heard a door open and footsteps approaching but she was too absorbed in the paintings to turn round. Someone came to the doorway.

'Given you some kitchen help at last, have they, Olive? About time.'

'Yes, a little treasure!' she heard Olive laugh.

'Tell your little treasure not to leave her wet stockings on the work top. It's most unhygenic.'

Laurie froze. She had recognised the voice and then the tall, burly figure in the doorway. Was he haunting her, following her around? And he had meant her to hear that last remark. Now at last she was going to meet the man and find out exactly who he was and what he was doing here. She had always had sparky courage, except that once—she pushed the mental torment to the back of her mind—then it had been too late for bravery.

'I'm sorry about the wet socks,' she said. 'I'll give the top an extra scrub down with Lysol. If you like, I could fumigate the whole kitchen.'

The flow of sarcasm stopped when she saw her adversary. She almost laughed. He was in a far worse state than she. His jacket was covered in mud, dark hair plastered to his head, heavy boots coated with slime and bits of fern. His eyes looked gaunt and weary, yet there was still plenty of fight left in him.

She knew he had taken in her bare feet, her slim figure and the way her thin shirt clung damply to her feminine curves. His mouth twitched with amusement. There were two bloodied scratches across his cheek and a dark stubble softened the hard line of his jaw. He grinned at both their disreputable appearances and in an odd way Laurie found that moment of unity immensely appealing.

'Is that something else you are quite good at?' he enquired, echoing her own words about reversing.

Olive came bustling back with a mug of tea. 'Here you are, Mr Ben, get this down you. Those daft walkers. Always getting themselves in trouble. Just as well there are a few people who know what they are doing on the fells.'

Laurie remembered his angry words in the drive about an emergency. It didn't take much imagination now to work out where he had been going.

'Was this rescue work?' she asked. 'Are you with a mountain rescue team?'

'Yes, that's where I was going when you decided to block the drive with your banger. Two walkers out on the fells. They had fallen in the mist. Fortunately one of them managed to get back to raise help.'

'Were they hurt?'

'Only one—a broken leg and collar-bone. He was

pretty bad and suffering from exposure.'

'I suppose the other walker knew nothing about how to immobilise broken bones? He left his friend to lay there in agony.'

The man raised his dark eyebrows at her comment. 'No, they had no idea and they had nothing with them for a night out on the hills. No protective clothing or equipment. They were wearing damned fool wind-cheaters with slogans and badges, sneakers and jeans suitable for a steamer trip on the lake.'

He followed Laurie out into the kitchen, making her all the more aware of his close scrutiny. His eyes were riveted on her. She picked up bowls of natural yoghurt, nuts and raisins to carry through to the dining-room. The hot tea had relaxed him and he had obviously decided to enjoy himself at her expense.

'No sticky buns for breakfast?' he queried, leaning against the counter, his long body twisted awkwardly.

'Strictly for midnight feasts.'

'It all looks very healthy and packed full of vitamins. I'm almost sorry I'm not staying. But then I'm a bacon and eggs man myself with lashings of crisply fried bread, tomatoes and mushrooms.'

Laurie's salivary glands hungered for such a treat. Occasionally she allowed herself a fry-up, but not often. She was pretty strict with her diet.

'Far too much cholesterol,' she murmured.

'What long words you use,' he said. 'Were you born with a dictionary in your chubby little hand?'

She ignored his remarks, busying herself with laying the breakfast table. She was used to working at speed and it was soon finished. She stuffed her wet pop socks in her pocket. Perhaps Olive could show her the accommodation soon. Weariness was sweeping over her in waves.

'Have you driven a long way?' he asked.

'I don't believe I said,' Laurie replied, stiffling a yawn. She had no intention of prolonging the conversation. The man was a mystery and he could stay that way. He was doing his best to be pleasant, but she was aware that beneath the charm lay a tough and precise character.

'Since our paths have crossed somewhat during this night, I'm curious about your coincidental arrival at Cumthwaite Hall.'

'Not coincidental at all. I was expected.'

'So now, little treasure, tell me about yourself. What are you doing here at this revolutionary school for solving all human problems? Are you kitchen maid or student, seeking insight into the wisdom of healing at the feet of a master?'

Laurie did not like the sudden scorn in his voice. She knew immediately that he was one of those awkward, narrow-minded people who would not even listen to new ideas or methods.

'Neither,' she said, drawing her full five foot four up with graceful dignity. Even in bare feet she had something, a correct balance which made her spine something quite beautiful to behold. 'I'm a teacher. My name is Laurie Young. I'm starting work at the School of Alexander Technique. I am fully qualified· but that doesn't mean I wouldn't help Olive if she's pushed for time. I'm perfectly willing to help her too.'

'A teacher, eh? One of those,' he drawled, taking in her plait and youthful appearance. 'I thought they had to do a three year course. When did you start? At thirteen or fourteen?'

'I'm well aware that you have a habit of looking but not seeing,' said Laurie. 'But I am twenty-six and actually age has nothing to do with appearance. It's behaviour that counts. I've met grown men, around thirty-six say, who are so juvenile and childish that one is surprised they are not wearing short pants.'

She thought for a moment that he was going to explode. And he did, but it was not with fury. He dissolved into deep laughter, his eyes glinting with merriment.

'What a firebrand, little miss teacher,' he grinned. 'You've a tongue like a laser beam, since dragons are outdated. I shall have to keep out of your way. That won't be difficult since I don't live at Cumthwaite Hall.'

Good, thought Laurie, hoping the relief did not show on her face. He didn't have anything to do with the school. Then she wouldn't be seeing him. Hardly ever, if he only cadged free drinks on his way back from rescuing people on the moors. She wondered about his part in the rescue work; what was his special skill. Glancing at his powerful shoulders, she decided it was sheer brawn.

Dragons and laser beams . . . had he somehow read her thoughts? It was disconcerting to think he might have seen some way into her mind. She did not want anyone to know what was there.

'The times we turn out for these badly equipped and ill-prepared people,' he was saying to Olive. 'They never learn. You'd think even an idiot would wear stout boots and waterproofs. The weather on the fells and high moors can change so quickly.'

'You'll be away to your bed then, Mr Ben,' said Olive soothingly. 'For what's left of the night.'

'Thanks for the tea, Olive. I'm due at Carlisle County at nine o'clock for a meeting. Barely time to put my head down.'

He dismissed Laurie with a brief nod, handing her the empty mug as he strode out. If he had not been so weary from the rescue operation, Laurie would have thrust the mug right back into his hand and told him to carry it out himself. But she recognised extreme fatigue and wondered how on earth he was going to drive to Carlisle in that state.

Before she knew what she was doing, she had run out on to the gravelled courtyard, and put a restraining hand on his arm. He turned, grey eyes barely focusing on her, as if he was unaware she was still around.

'You're so quick at handing out the good advice, why not let me drive you to Carlisle,' she offered impulsively. 'You're in no fit state——'

He looked incredulous. 'Drive me? In that sardine can of yours?'

Laurie ignored the slur on her car. 'In my vintage Austin,' she corrected. 'Have *you* got walnut picnic trays?'

'You haven't slept either.'

'I had a nap in the car when I got here, then a brisk early morning walk by the lake. I'm as fresh as a daisy.'

He took a closer look at her, his breath fanning her cheek. 'Petals drooping, I should say. No, thank you, I don't trust flower power. Besides, I've my own driver coming.'

Laurie felt her back stiffen at the rebuff. She had to consciously loosen and lengthen her spine to let go of the tension. So he was an influential man with a driver at his disposal. So what? She had not wanted to go to Carlisle anyway. She wanted to unpack, have a bath and find her bearings in this new environment.

'Good. So you're all right then,' she said dismissively, turning away.

He caught her arm roughly and pulled her back. A wave of alarm and fear raced through her. He bent, touching her cheek curiously with the tip of his finger. The contact was like an electric shock. He traced the line from her cheek bone down to her pointed jaw, stopping at the small indentation of a dimple. Her skin tingled with apprehension. Panic began to rise, yet her fear was

mingled with another new and different response from
her body. Her eyes widened as he came nearer, but she
was transfixed. She could not move. He planted a small,
moist kiss on the corner of her full mouth and lingered
momentarily. Then he drew away with a vague
expression of regret.

'That was a thank you,' he said. 'It was a kind thought
to offer to drive a crusty old climber who does not deserve
the time of day. I apologise for not being more
appreciative. You've been travelling all night too and
should be tucked up in your bed like a good little girl.'

Laurie was thrown by his sudden change to gentleness
and a certain rough charm. Her wits deserted her and she
was lost for words. She could only think of the tantalising
closeness of his lean body and how her heart was
pounding like a wild thing in her chest.

'It was you at the motorway cafeteria, wasn't it?' she
croaked.

'Yes, I was driving back from London.'

'I thought you were a truck driver. I thought you were
trying to pick me up.'

'Ah . . .' he said, non-committally.

'You looked like a truck driver,' she insisted, some of
her natural spirit returning. 'Scruffy jeans and leather
jacket.'

'I had a puncture. I had to change a tyre on the hard
shoulder. And I wasn't trying to pick you up. I was
concerned when I saw what I thought was a runaway
teenager stuffing herself with a sticky bun. I wanted to
warn you before it was too late.'

'It was a doughnut.'

His eyes clouded, an edge of irritability eroding the
Good Samaritan. His good nature obviously had a very
short fuse. 'I don't care what it was. I just thought you
might have been in trouble and needed some help.'

'Well, I didn't.'

'It's nice to know you are so grateful,' he growled. 'One of the old-fashioned type. Most modern girls don't even know the meaning of the word.'

'Girls today don't have much to be grateful for in this modern world,' she said valiantly. 'It can be a cruel place, and being physically weaker, we're easy targets.'

'Oh dear,' he mocked. 'Do I detect bitterness? In one so young? Have you been let down by some man?'

He could not have chosen more unfortunate words. Laurie was over-tired and afterwards she could only use that as an excuse. Without thinking, she swung round, a fury of pent-up anger and frustration so openly on her face that she did not seem the same person. Her stiffened hand caught him sharply across the cheek. It was a blow, not meant for him but for other faceless men who had taunted her with almost the same words.

He drew in a gasp of surprise and pain. Red weal marks immediately appeared on his face. They looked at each other in total shock. His eyes hardened to granite and Laurie could only stare at him, aghast.

'I . . . I'm . . . ' she breathed, backing from him.

He put his hand to his face, gingerly touching the weals. 'I believe you've drawn blood.'

Laurie fought for breath, for control and composure. She thought she had come to terms with that horrific night, but a few ill-chosen words had shown how exposed were her nerves. Her reaction had been purely physical. She had not frozen with fear this time. A reflex action, way beyond any mental control, had been triggered off, shocking both of them.

'Do you always attack totally strange men?' he said, punching the words savagely. Laurie felt humiliated by his venom, yet acknowledged that he had done nothing to deserve the blow. There was no way she could explain to him. How could she? It was a secret that had to remain hidden from the world.

'I didn't mean it,' she said, her voice barely a whisper. 'I don't know why . . . it was like someone else moving my hand, not me at all. It's never happened before.'

'I'm glad to hear it. Hysterical women are not part of the scene around here, and I've no time to waste in analysing your motive, however devious.'

'I am trying to apologise. You could listen to me and not interrupt. It isn't easy to try and explain irrational behaviour.'

She was hopelessly aware of his dark presence stamping its identity on her soul. Even in those moments of despair, she knew her fingers longed to curl into the dark hair at the nape of his neck. She longed to breath his skin, to lose herself in his strong arms, to pretend she was safe and had no fear of the future. But no man could provide that. No man was a safe haven.

'If this is how teachers of the Alexander Technique behave, then heaven help the students here,' he said evenly. 'I think we'll pretend this has never happened, that it's part of a bad night all round. If we ever meet again and I certainly hope we don't, it will be as if for the first time. I will forget this incident and so will you. But I must say that you are a poor advertisement for any method of healing, and it simply reinforces my opinion that people like you live in a fantasy of your own making, cut off from the real world.'

Laurie was trying to master a crushing disappointment, a devastating failure in herself. She had been doing so well, and then to let herself down with such a stupid reaction.

'I'm so sorry . . . it was something you said,' she began again in a low voice. But he was not listening. She felt so wretched; she wanted him to understand without being told why she had acted that way. She preferred his anger to this icy contempt.

'Don't bother with any excuses,' he snapped. 'I'm not interested.'

He strode across the courtyard to his car, got in and started the engine, driving away in a wide sweep of spurting gravel. Laurie stood on the step, shaking, tears close to the surface. What had she done? She had hardly even started her new work and already she had antagonised someone who had no time for the Alexander Technique or it principles.

The day was lightening rapidly now and the mist evaporating as the air warmed. Cumthwaite Hall appeared before her like some fairy-tale Disney set, its grey stone walls bathed in soft morning light that was reflected in the myriads of glass in the handsome Tudor windows and the delicate oriel window over the front entrance. Creepers wove long strands of web-like fingers along the South facing wall, shrouding the dormer windows in the roof with greenery. The crenallated turret roof stood boldly against the sky, the clusters of ornate chimneys like birthday candles waiting to be lit.

Laurie felt some of the tension ease. Acres of peace. It was romantically old, guarded by trees to one side and the lake on the other. The home of Benedictine nuns, James Robinson had said. She wished their devotion could help her now. Perhaps some of their prayers had rubbed off on the walls or still echoed in the wavelengths surrounding the building. She looked upwards. Was that her turret, that square area high on the roof? She hoped it was. It looked like a refuge.

She unpacked a few bags from her car and carried them indoors through the kitchen entrance. Olive had finished preparing the breakfast and was clearing the work surfaces.

'I've told Mr Robinson that you've arrived. He's gone out jogging round the lake. He does a couple of miles every morning. He says you're to make yourself at home and he'll see you around lunchtime. I've the key to your little flat.'

'Great,' said Laurie. 'I'll take these things up and come back for the rest later.'

Laurie followed her through to the main hall. It was warm and mellow with a high, vaulted ceiling and a wealth of polished panelling, another big fireplace, and a richly carved oak staircase wide enough for ladies in their farthingales to make splendid entrances. Its treads were covered in worn dark red carpet that matched the lampshades over the mantelpiece and the upholstery of the high-backed chairs placed facing the fire. The stained glass from the oriel window threw rainbow rays into the lofty space giving the ornate carving lightness and warmth.

Olive's broad back trudged up the stairs and along a carved screened gallery towards numerous corridors branching off, then another flight of carpeted stairs till finally she rested at the foot of some narrow stairs which Laurie guessed were the ones too steep for the guests.

'I'll leave you now,' Olive puffed. 'Up these stairs. Door at the top. You can't miss it. Help yourself to anything for breakfast if you want it.'

'Thanks, but no. I'm past eating. I just want to sleep.'

Olive gave her the key and smiled. 'See you tomorrow then, bright and perky.'

'Thanks again,' said Laurie. 'You've been very kind. I'm really grateful. I'm sorry I wasn't much help.'

'Never you mind. I'm useless too if I don't get my eight hours.'

Laurie paused on the bottom step, hoisting a bag over her shoulder. She did not care really, didn't even want to

know, but she hated mysteries and could not stop herself
from asking.

'Who was that man? The one who had been out
rescuing the fell walkers?'

Olive's smile creased even wider. 'Why, that's Mr
Ben. Well, that's what I always call him, I've known him
since he was a boy. But he's a professor now, Professor
Reuben Vaughan, with a string of letters after his name.
Perhaps you've heard of him. He's quite famous in a
way, goes round the world lecturing—an expert he is on
drugs. Not drug addicts, mind you, not that kind. But
something to do with the NHS and prescriptions.'

'Do you mean he lectures to medical audiences on
adverse drug reactions?' Laurie said faintly.

'Yes, that's it in a nutshell. Why, you know more about
it than I do. It must be your training.'

It was her training all right, thought Laurie, and she
ought to know more about it. She had a vague feeling she
had even been to one of his rare lectures to trainee nurses.
If she checked through her old notes, she felt sure she
would find his name, Professor Vaughan. He was an
eminent man in the medical profession and the last person
she should have annoyed. Though she had to remind
herself that she had left the profession and the whole lot of
them were ordinary people again, not gods and demi-
gods. Still she would make sure she never saw him again.
She would keep out of his way.

'Does he live around here?' she asked.

'Bless you, yes. When he's at home, and that's not
often. He lives in the Boathouse, down by the lake. All
converted it is into a bachelor pad, very modern and
comfortable. Wouldn't do for me though; all that lapping
water outside would keep me awake. But he likes it. His
hide-away, he calls it. Doesn't like visitors.'

Laurie's heart fell still further. How could she keep

a low profile if he lived in the grounds? They would be always bumping into each other, or their cars would. It was hard enough making this fresh start without all these further complications.

'But he's hardly ever there,' said Olive finally. 'If I see him twice in the same month, I think it's Christmas. Never known anyone for so much travelling. They don't see much of him at Carlisle County either, even though he's on the staff.'

'Ah, Carlisle County Hospital?'

'That's right. Where our fell walker will be right now. Helicoptered him in, right off the moors. Wonderful what they do these days, isn't it?'

Laurie nodded with a smile she didn't really feel. She struggled up the narrow stairs, bags bumping against her thighs and knees. There was a glassed-in door at the top. She wondered how much of a flatlet they had managed to make out of the turret space. She opened the door and found herself in a big square room with windows on three sides. She dropped the bags and ran to each of them in turn. The first looked down into the courtyard and across to the wall covered in creeper, the second gazed back at the rolling hills and distant brown crags and the third gave her an uninterrupted view of the lawns sloping down to the tree-studded lakeside. Beyond the trees the water glittered like a mirror, too early yet to be disturbed by the wash of steamers.

It was so idyllic and peaceful. Laurie leaned her arms on the wide windowsill and drank in the view. She had not realised that the Lake District was so lovely. Passionate tranquillity . . . where had she heard that? It was one of the poets, but which one?

The room was simply furnished with a single divan, a desk and backless posture stool, fitted clothes cupboard, and two big tapestry bean bags for sitting on instead of armchairs. No broken collapses into upholstered loungers were allowed at Cumthwaite Hall—Laurie smiled.

An alcove lead off to the smallest kitchen Laurie had ever seen. It was caravan size with a miniscule washing-up bowl, two electric hot plates and a tiny refrigerator no bigger than a drinks cupboard. She examined it all with delight, opening doors and drawers. There was everything she could need to be self-sufficient. The bathroom next door was even smaller with only just enough room to turn round between the shower and the wash basin. But it was all hers. Laurie felt her spirits lifting. She would go shopping in Windermere and buy herself a few extras. And once she had unpacked her things, the turret would really feel like a home.

Laurie let herself down on to the floor into the semi-supine position, adjusting a few paperbacks under her head, flexing her bent knees till they were in the right position and the sacrum was comfortably placed on the carpet. She let out a small groan. She needed this after the long night's drive stuck behind a steering wheel. Those poor, compressed discs in her spine were crying out for the vital fluid. She centred her mind on the pressure points of her body against the floor, back of her head on the books, shoulders flat on the floor with bent elbows spread out, sacrum, fleshless and hard, heels, ball of the foot, big toes.

Gradually she became more aware of the world outside and listened deliberately, keeping in touch—twittering bird song, wind rustling through the branches, something tapping on a windowpane, the drone of an aeroplane in the stratosphere.

Her thoughts drifted to Reuben Vaughan. They shouldn't, she knew. This wasn't day-dream time. But he was there, in her mind, everything about him, a disturbing image like unwanted shadows, strong and

masculine and undeniably attractive despite their war of
words. If only . . . but wishful thinking was futile. She had
managed to ruin any normal friendship which might have
been possible.

Laurie fell asleep on the floor, at some point rolling
over and pulling the patterned duvet off the bed to cover
herself. Her last thoughts were of a man, tall and dark,
kissing her mouth with a gentleness that could have begun
the healing of her bruised heart.

CHAPTER THREE

THE NATIONAL Trust land near Bowness Nab ferry was a promontory of shady woodland with a path that led down to a narrow beach. Laurie was surprised to see people sunbathing on the sloping sand and children playing at the water's edge as if they were at the seaside. She strolled along enjoying the general holiday feeling and letting the sun warm her arms.

This was her first afternoon off from the School at Cumthwaite Hall. It had been a hectic week with much to learn and many new people to meet; every bit as confusing as a big hospital. But the routine was totally different to NHS medicine and there was a relaxed atmosphere that encouraged Laurie not to worry about her mistakes.

Mornings began with everyone enjoying the large buffet breakfast, a spread of healthy wholemeal foods and fruits that delighted Laurie, used as she was to soggy hospital cornflakes and burnt bacon. The first classes were a general session of loosening up and relaxation, of ring songs and simple forms of line dancing. New students found this part of the activities rather difficult and there was much embarrassed laughing at first. But it was all calculated to assist in leaving the present world and its troubles behind, and clearing the mind. Next came a lecture on anatomy and the theory of the Alexander Technique by James Robinson, followed by the practical work in which Laurie and the three others teachers took the students in turn for individual tuition and manual guidance.

Laurie soon found that a few students were booking afternoon lessons with her and this was very gratifying, James also generously recommended a few private patients to her and Laurie's free time dwindled as she became busier.

She also discovered that she was still learning, even though she was a qualified teacher. James was bursting with enthusiasm for the Alexander Technique and his living example was an inspiration. His lectures were full of lively wisdom and Laurie made sure not to miss any, even if she was not expected to attend.

Her three colleagues were kind and helpful. Melanie was an airy-fairy creature who lived in a cottage near Ambleside and danced barefoot like a flower girl while Tamsin was a cool, composed young woman with a touch of the oriental about her. She lived in Windermere and cycled in each morning. The third teacher, Faith, was an older woman but still slim and her face unlined, a perfect advertisement for the technique. Laurie was not yet sure where Faith lived, but she suspected it was with James who had a flat over the stables and garage.

She flung herself down on the grassy bank and watched the children playing on the sand. The Bowness Nab ferry shunted backwards and forwards from one side of the lake to the other, taking a full load of cars on each journey. Sunlight sparkled on the water, breaking into mirror fragments that danced on the lapping waves. Boats were moored along the water's edge, bobbing gently. It was very attractive and peaceful, so undemanding. Already Laurie felt some of the tension and strain leaving her body.

Her car was off the road temporarily. The fuel gauge was not working. But the lack of wheels had not deterred her and she had taken the bus into Windermere and walked down the leafy hill to Bowness. She leaned back and closed her eyes, though she could still see the sun's rays through her eyelids. She could hear skylarks singing with joy. If only everything could be as simple as these moments here.

A dog was barking, sharp excited yelps as it pranced around a boy building a sand-castle. Its paws were kicking up sprays of sand in the air, showering the boy and his castle.

'Stop it, Rex! Stop it. Bad dog! You're getting in my way!'

The dog redoubled its efforts at digging, mistaking the words for unexpected encouragement. The boy began to laugh, but his mirth suddenly changed to screams as grains of sand flew into his eyes. He started to cry and rub his eyes, running to his mother.

Laurie sat up, watching the scene. The child was very distressed and his mother was not helping much, shouting at the dog and trying to peer into the boy's eyes at the same time. Laurie hurried over, opening her shoulder bag to find a clean handkerchief.

'Can I help?' she said quickly. 'I know what to do.'

'He's got sand in his eyes. That damned dog. I'll kill it.'

'You can't blame the dog,' said Laurie. 'Don't rub your eyes, young man. Hold your son's arms down, will you?' she said to the mother. 'He's only making things worse by rubbing.'

Laurie turned the boy round so that he was facing the light, his face stained with tears, his eyes reddened. She pulled down the lower lid gently and removed the particles with a corner of the handkerchief. The boy wriggled and twisted in discomfort.

'Please keep still,' said Laurie in a firm voice.

'Keep still you little wretch,' snapped his mother.

'I can't help you if you keep jigging around. Look, the sand's coming out. Let's do the other one and it'll stop hurting.'

It was more difficult to raise the upper eyelid, although the boy's tears were helping to wash out the sand. Laurie knew he ought to have his eyes properly cleansed in case any sand or dirt was embedded in the eyeball.

'I think you should take your son to the Casualty Department of the local hospital. Have you got a car? They'll examine his eyes and put in some soothing drops.'

'All right. I suppose I'd better take him, then. What an afternoon! Stop that crying, can't you? It's getting on my nerves.' The flustered mother tried to pack up their belongings.

'Let him cry,' said Laurie, helping to collect bags and buckets. 'Tears are slightly antiseptic.'

The little party were staggering up the slope, hampered by Rex still excitedly leaping around and getting in everyone's way, when Laurie was aware of a familiar figure striding towards them. It was Ben Vaughan looking more like a truck driver than ever in dark jeans and a sweat-shirt, bulky and bear-like, his eyes quickly assessing the situation.

His glance moved over her too, taking in the strappy thin cotton top and flowered skirt, her glossy hair loose on her shoulders and bare feet in sandals. Laurie found her heart racing at the sight of him in a way that did not make any sense, yet she wished him a thousand miles away.

'What's the matter?' he asked. 'I spotted you from the queue for the ferry.'

She tried to slip past him, but he stopped her just as he had in the motorway café by standing squarely in front of her. She evaded his eyes, suddenly embarrassed and awkward, unable to find anything witty or intelligent to say.

'Nothing's the matter. Everything's under control. Now if you'll excuse us . . . we're in a hurry.'

'I saw what happened. Did the boy get sand in his eyes?'

'If you saw, then why ask?'

'I was interested in the way you coped. You seemed to know what you were doing.'

'Simple first aid, Mr Vaughan,' said Laurie. 'Nothing special. Anyone could have done it. The mother is taking the boy to Casualty now.'

He nodded, but she suspected he was finding some amusement in the situation. 'Very wise,' he agreed. 'It's always sensible to have eyes checked by an expert.'

He tipped the boy's face gently and peered at the inflamed eyes. 'Lucky for you that Miss Young was around, young man. You'll soon be as right as rain. And when they've looked at you in Casualty, you'll be able to take your mother out for a slap-up tea with strawberries and cream and chocolate cake. How about that?'

Ben Vaughan slipped a note into the boy's shirt pocket and gave him a push in the direction of the car park. The mother thanked Ben, stuttering over her words, then thanked Laurie again for her help.

Ben took Laurie's arm and steered her away from the family, not listening to her protest. He was making his way purposefully towards the car ferry and now Laurie could see why. His metallic Mercedes was blocking the queue and the cars behind him were wanting to move into the loading lane.

'Is this your afternoon off?' he asked interrupting.

'Yes, it is, so if you don't mind, I'd like to be on my way. I've things to do.'

'What things?'

'You wouldn't be interested.'

'Try me. I'm interested.'

He was laughing at her again. Laurie snatched her arm away and jammed her bag firmly on her shoulder. She was trembling with annoyance at his attitude.

'Please don't be patronising, Mr Vaughan. I'm well

aware that you are an eminent man in your field and it
was very kind of you to come over. The boy's accident
was hardly life-threatening so your expertise was not
really required. However, since you are about to lose
your place in the ferry queue, you'd better get going.'

She felt the colour warm in her cheeks. Never in her
hospital days would she have spoken to a consultant in
such a way. Although she had often got into trouble for
being outspoken, she had always held senior staff in great
respect. This was a new Laurie Young speaking and it
gave her goose-prickles under the skin.

He did not look particulary pleased and for a second his
grey eyes cooled. But then he realised what it must have
cost her to be so frighteningly honest and he could only
admire her for it. People did not often talk to him straight.
Mostly they said what they thought he wanted to hear.'

'I didn't mean to interfere, I'm sorry. Come for a
drive. I could do with some company. I'm going to
Hawkshead. It's quaint and pretty, though a little
battered by the thousand of tourists who troop there to see
the cottage where Wordsworth lodged when he went to
the Grammar School.'

He held open the car door. He rarely apologised to
anyone. It was a new experience and it surprised him.
What was it about this elfin girl with her soft hazel eyes
that at one and the same time could infuriate him and also
fill him with waves of protectiveness? He dismissed such
thoughts quickly as Laurie turned to make her escape.
She had no intention of going anywhere with him.
Bowness would do quite nicely for her first afternoon off.
It might not be very adventurous but it was definitely less
complicated.

'No, please don't go,' he urged. 'I'm going to see a
friend, a painter. You were admiring her paintings in
Cumthwaite Hall. She paints the Cumbrian landscape in

a very special way.'

Laurie backed against the body of the car. Someone was hooting impatiently at the big estate blocking the way on to the ferry. She was beginning to feel hot and tired but her interest was stirred. The paintings at the Hall were beautiful and she had been admiring them all week. And Professor Vaughan knew the painter. She was a friend. That was the kind of circle he moved in. This was the shape and level of his life . . . lecturing at leading hospitals, here and abroad; of knowing important and influential people in many spheres; being a vital link in a mountain rescue team. For a second it made her feel small and insignificant, but her independent spirit came to the rescue; her new career was important in a different way.

'Her paintings are wonderful. I really like them,' said Laurie. 'And I'd love to meet her. Thank you.'

She slid into his car and closed the door before he could change his mind. He manoeuvred the big car on to the ferry and Laurie felt a welcome breeze on her face as it began to clank slowly across the lake, pulling itself on two chains. It was a short water crossing taking about seven minutes, but still there was a small thrill of excitement. She must go on a trip on a lake steamer and see for herself all the beauty of the wooded shores.

. She sat back to enjoy the roominess of the car compared to her small Austin. Ben Vaughan was a good driver despite their encounter in the drive of Cumthwaite Hall and Laurie found she was able to relax and admire the countryside sliding by. The sweet bracken and spruce tree scents wafted through the open windows.

Hawkshead was a picturesque village dominated by a huge car-park. It had been designated a no-traffic area, but the planners had put the necessary car-park near the centre. Laurie thought it was still a magical village with seventeenth century timber framed inns and cobbled

courtyards, really old cottages built round squares that
were not square; every lane revealing quaint steps and
overhanging archways.

'There are, of course, far too many tourists.' said Ben,
striding through the crowds. 'Wordsworth is simply an
industry these days. Half of them won't have the remotest
idea who he was, let alone have actually read his poems.'

'They aren't doing any harm,' said Laurie defensively.
'And I'm a tourist this afternoon. I even learned one of
his poems at school.'

'Daffodils . . . lonely clouds etc.'

'No, the Immortality Ode. ''There was a time when
meadow, grove, and stream, the earth, and every
common sight, to me did seem apparell'd in celestial
light'',' she quoted, then faltered. She did not want to risk
drying up. 'I must buy a few postcards. This is lovely and
they've done the right thing, keeping out the cars.'

'They didn't keep them out far enough,' he grunted.
'This is Priscilla's cottage, White Moss. Come on in.'

The tiny cottage was perfect. A carefully restored
plaster and weathered oak dwelling, bow-windows under
thatched eaves; creepers climbing the rickety porch and
the garden a tangle of roses and weeds. Ben pushed open
a creaking gate and it seemed to Laurie that a lot of
tenseness left him as he entered the garden. The perfume
from the blown roses was heady, and Laurie knew
instinctively that Priscilla was going to be as perfect as her
cottage and her garden.

Laurie heard her laugh before she saw the woman. It
was low and musical and the woman who followed the
sound was quite beautiful. She was pale skinned and
ethereal with silvery hair that tangled on her shoulders;
eyes that glowed like her own paintings, lips sweetly
curved and feminine. Some sort of thin robe floated round
her in a muted rainbow of colours. She put her arms up to

Ben and kissed him warmly.

'Ben . . . what a lovely surprise. I never see you these days. It's been ages.'

'All of six weeks,' he gently mocked.

She wrinkled her nose delicately. 'Is that all? It seems years, but you know what I'm like when I'm working. Time means nothing. But you're here now and I'm not going to let you go. Come and see what I'm working on. I've discovered the volcanic rocks and I can't stop painting them.'

Laurie scraped the heel of her sandal on the path. Priscilla turned and looked at her in surprise.

'Hello,' she said. 'Oh dear, are you lost or something?'

'This is Laurie Young,' said Ben. 'I've brought her to see you. She has been admiring your paintings at Cumthwaite Hall and couldn't resist the chance of meeting you.'

It was a slight exaggeration of the truth but Laurie let it go. Priscilla was very beautiful, Laurie conceded generously. She was as elegant and lovely as a white peacock. She made Laurie feel like a small brown dove beside her. No doubt the comparison had not escaped Ben.

'I'm sorry. I thought you were a tourist. We are always getting lost ones wandering into the garden. So are you a member of Ben's fraternity at the hospital?' Priscilla smiled and welcomed Laurie into the garden. She motioned Laurie to sit beside her on a wooden bench, draping her long thin skirts round her knees.

'Heavens no,' said Ben answering for her. 'I doubt if Miss Young could stand the sight of blood. Her constitution is obviously of a squeamish nature.'

Little do you know, buster, Laurie longed to say. 'Heavens no,' she echoed. 'I would just pass out. I'm not one of the blood and gore brigade.'

'Nor me! Remember when I put a skewer through my thumb at a barbecue, Ben? I fainted on the spot. Some party!'

Ben took Priscilla's thumb into his hand and turned it gently, pouring over the scrolls and whirls.

'There is the tiniest scar,' she added in a low voice that was meant just for him.

Laurie squirmed. She saw all the signs, the soft eyes, the yearning; they had almost forgotten she was present. She would leave them and look around the village.

'So are you on holiday, Miss Young,' said Priscilla suddenly remembering her visitor.

'No, I'm living at Cumthwaite Hall, teaching. It's a School of the Alexander Technique now. We take residential students as well as doing private work.'

'Oh yes, the Alexander Technique. I've heard of it. Sort of relaxation, isn't it?'

'Don't pretend it has any viability, Priscilla,' said Ben, stretching out on the grass. 'It's a load of rubbish. Fringe stuff. A cult.'

Laurie swallowed her anger. They were taught never to rise to baiting. It was a basic lesson, and particularly hard to keep to when the tormentor was completely ignorant.

'It's difficult to put into a nutshell,' said Laurie. 'I often wish there were a few pat phrases I could trot out and all would be explained. Matthias Alexander pioneered the technique as long ago as the mid-1890s. He discovered that posture and muscular tension could be the cause of many common complaints of breathing, digestion, headaches, back-pain, mental stress, neuromuscular and joint problems.'

'Spare us a list,' Ben grunted, eyes closed to the sun.

'We try to help people change the continual misuse of their bodies, undo bad habits often learned in childhood and copied from adults, or new ones arising from habits at work.'

'Good posture in other words,' Priscilla put in.

'It's not even that. In fact the parade-ground back straight and head up stresses the neck and tips the head back unnaturally. It creates misalignment and deformity. If only schools could have regular Alexander Technique lessons, then in a few years, half of our hospitals and surgeries would be empty!'

'What a splendid idea,' said Ben, folding his arms behind his neck. 'I would have more time for sailing.'

He was not taking it seriously. Laurie longed to shake his complacency and make him listen. Even now, stretched out on the grass, he was not completely relaxed. She could see tension in his neck. She wondered what he would do if she knelt behind him and gently stretched that neck into a more natural position?

'It's your kind of opinionated intolerances that keeps the medical profession in the Middle Ages,' said Laurie quietly. 'We should be talking together, listening to each other, working alongside patients, not being at loggerheads all the time.'

'The Middle Ages! Hey, that's a bit steep, What about insulin, antibiotics, anaesthetics, transplants? Don't they count for anything? Or are you claiming that the Alexander Technique has an alternative answer for progress? I'll send you along a couple of broken legs and some brain surgery,' he jeered.

'Of course I'm not claiming we can mend broken bones or supersede surgery, and there have been wonderful new discoveries in medicine. But we can reshape the quality of life after an illness or operation, and in many cases the Alexander Technique might have prevented the necessity for surgery or drugs in the first place.'

'Professor dear, watch out! You're under fire from this bright young woman,' Priscilla laughed. 'She's determined to make you see the light.'

'I'd sooner take to the hills and be a hermit,' he said.

'I think it's fascinating,' said Priscilla. 'Do you think your school could do anything for my right shoulder? It does hurt after a long day.'

Laurie forced her mind away from Ben. She was really seething at his attitude. What an achievement if she could get him to acknowledge that the Alexander Technique had a place in modern day medicine. But it was impossible when he was so stubborn and arrogant. She turned her attention to the lovely artist, noting the way she sat, the tilt of her head.

'It might be something to do with your working methods. I'd have to see how you stand at your easel. Perhaps there's tension you're unaware of when you hold a brush, or a stiffening of your head.'

'I didn't know your shoulder was giving you trouble,' Ben interrupted. 'I'll make an appointment for you at physiotherapy.'

'No, you won't. I haven't got time. I haven't even got time to take an aspirin. Everything is so fleeting and I must capture it all on canvas before it disappears.'

'Cumbria will be around a little longer,' said Ben. 'You wanted to show me some new work?'

'Oh Ben, I just don't know about it. Volcanic rock—it's so exciting but I might be on the wrong track . . .'

They began to talk art, of Priscilla's doubts and hopes. Ben was listening, absorbed, his chin resting on his hand.

'I think I'll take a look at the village,' said Laurie, rising from the bench in a single fluid movement.

Priscilla held out her hand with a smile, long silver-tipped fingers waving at Laurie. 'Bye, then. I'm very pleased to have met you. I'm glad you like my paintings.' She turned back to Ben, dismissing Laurie with a slight flick of silvery hair. 'Come along, Ben. I want to show you my new work.'

Laurie accepted the dismissal with good-humour. 'Don't worry about me. I'll wander around the village and buy my postcards like any normal tourist. I'll be very good and I won't write on the walls or throw litter about.'

Priscilla looked amused. She raised her delicate eyebrows at Ben. He patted her arm reassuringly and Laurie was momentarily jarred by his intimate manner. She did not seem to know what she wanted. She certainly did not want him, and yet she did envy their close relationship. Well, she had left it far too late to be nice to him now. She might just as well accept that and put him out of her mind.

'Laurie has an odd sense of humour. It might be possible to get used to it in time. Come back in an hour, Laurie, and I'll take you to see Beatrix Potter's house at Sawrey. It's near here.'

'What more sightseeing?' said Laurie with mock astonishment. 'Can I stand it? All this culture in one afternoon. Lawks, sir, I shall be overcome with fatigue . . .'

Ben was hardly listening. He had quite forgotten her. His craggy face was in repose, his thoughts far from her rambling.

A pang shot through her as she caught the fleeting expression on Ben's face. He was looking at Priscilla with an unfathomable mixture of affection and admiration, envy and humility. Laurie could not understand why it should upset her. She did not know Ben Vaughan. She hardly knew if she liked him. It was obvious the two were more than friends—that Priscilla was older than Ben was of no consequence. In maturity, a few years age gap meant nothing.

'See you later,' she added brightly.

Hawkshead was cut off in time by the absence of cars. Laurie half expected to see a milkmaid coming round a corner with slopping pails, or an ancient cowman driving a couple of cows along one of the narrow lanes. Instead the tourists stood and gawped and took photographs. She wondered what the young Wordsworth would have made of all this.

Such wandering was a luxury for Laurie. She had never had this amount of time absolutely to herself like this in London. Most of her free time she had spent catching up on her sleep, or mending stockings, washing and ironing. The slanting sun reminded her that the afternoon was passing and shadows from the fells lengthened; sounds drifted down from the steep hills, thin reedy sheep bleats, a distant car changing gear, geese flying overhead, a dog barking.

For the first time in a week she thought about Bruce. This was what he needed, peace and space. Hospital life was killing him and he had mistakenly believed that Laurie was his salvation. In a rush of generosity, Laurie decided to invite him to Windermere for a weekend, for a break. He could stay at Cumthwaite Hall. She wanted to share all this with him, this great tract of land that stretched greenly in every direction, beautiful broad-leaved trees, dry stone walls and stiles, stone bridges over the rushing becks from the hills.

It took Laurie some time to find White Moss Cottage again for she had lost any sense of direction. Ben and Priscilla were waiting for her in the garden, sprawled on the tiny lawn, a jug of iced lemonade at their side, glasses in their hands. They looked contented and happy, and for once Ben seemed relaxed. He was dishevelled, his dark hair ruffled, sleeves rolled up over muscular arms. Laurie felt acutely embarrassed. She did not want to imagine how they had spent the last hour together.

'Have a drink,' Ben offered. 'You look hot.'

That means I look red and shiny, and a mess, thought

Laurie, accepting the drink. There was a third glass on the tray so at least she had been included in the refreshments.

'Did you have a nice stroll?' Priscilla asked.

'Very nice,' said Laurie.

'We'd better go then,' said Ben, pulling himself up with long, lazy grace. He held out a hand to Priscilla, and did not let go of it when she stood by his side. 'It's been lovely seeing you again. An afternoon away from all the stresses and strains. Thanks for everything.' His mouth brushed Priscilla's ear and Laurie almost choked on her lemonade.

'Don't let it be so long next time,' Priscilla chided.

'I doubt if you notice the days going by when you are painting,' he teased. 'So stop telling me off.'

Laurie wished she was miles away, and not a witness to this affectionate and playful exchange. She finished the drink in a gulp and put the glass down on the tray.

'Hey, it's time to go, I'm beginning to feel like a gooseberry,' she said. 'If this is a private conversation, I'd better disappear again.' How ridiculous, she thought. She would be better off getting a bus.

An expression of annoyance flashed across Ben's face. 'There's no need,' he said. 'It's the schoolmarm coming out—in force. She can't help it,' he said to Priscilla. 'Teachers probably have to clock in.'

Laurie was about to protest when she found herself being hustled out of the garden gate and down the lane with only a hurried goodbye to the artist. She tripped on a rough stone and the jolt nearly sent her flying. Her impact against Ben's thigh gave her a sudden insight into the unleashed power of his body. He was all man, and with that knowledge came a sense of her feminity and frailty. But it did not diminish her outrage at the way he was pushing her around.

'I'm no schoolmarm, thank you,' she gasped, shaking off his hand. 'So please don't refer to me in that patronising way. If that's what you think of other professions, especially all those hard-working teachers, then I'm surprised you haven't been lynched before now.'

'Don't you ever tell me what to do again,' he swung on her angrily. 'If I want to stay on with Priscilla, I will. It's none of your business what I do. Perhaps it was a mistake, bringing you here. I thought you would like to meet Priscilla.'

'So I did, and she's really nice. She listened,' Laurie muttered. 'Which is more than I can say for some people.'

'Now it seems you can't even be polite. I should have known better. It was an absurd impluse to bring you to Hawkshead, thinking you would enjoy it. We'd better get back to Cumthwaite Hall immediately. I've some lecture notes to put together for tomorrow and they can't wait. Phenothiazines are tricky.'

'The central nervous system,' said Laurie without thinking.

He shot her a quick glance. Laurie could have bitten her tongue. She had been caught off guard by the suddenness of his attack on her. 'Knowing about tranquillizers was part of my training as a teacher of the Alexander Technique,' she added, hoping he would believe her.

'Then you'll know the side-effects of phenothiazines are extremely common and can be serious, but I won't bore you with such details as tardive dyskinesias.' She had the feeling he was testing her, his penetrating eyes trying to see beyond her polite face.

'I'm so grateful,' said Laurie, her voice full of irony. 'I doubt if I have the intelligence to understand a single word. Ah, the car-park. I can't tell you how glad I am to see an ordinary car again. The sooner I get back to civilisation the better.'

'Get the bus if my company is so abhorrent,' he snapped.

'Okay, I will,' said Laurie, her temper rising. 'That'll suit me fine. Since you are in such a terrible hurry, I won't delay you a moment longer.'

'Ribble route 515,' he told her. 'Wednesdays only.'

'Right!'

She flung herself away, then stopped abruptly, her hand flying to her head in dismay. 'Wednesdays. What do you mean, Wednesdays only?'

He sighed elaborately which infuriated Laurie. He had no reason to be so unpleasant to her.

'The fourth day of the week, or the third day of the working week, whichever way you care to look at it,' he explained carefully as if to someone with low-grade English.

'You're impossible,' she said. 'As a matter of interest, do you find some pleasure in baiting me? I think you must, otherwise you wouldn't be so rude to me.'

'Get in,' he said, ignoring her outburst. 'Or perhaps you would prefer to walk to the ferry, then get a bus from Bowness?'

Laurie got into his car without another word. It was a long walk. She could not trust herself to speak. She could not understand how she had got herself into such a state. Her afternoon off was ruined. She wished she had never set eyes on him. Her initial clashes with him should have warned her. It was a lesson she must never forget.

She was trembling and that was unfair. It was not her fault. She tried to control her breathing, wishing she could find somewhere to lay down in a semi-supine position and calm herself. Instead she clasped her hands lightly in her lap and freed her shoulders from the tenseness.

She did not watch the scenery passing by. It was simply not registering as her thoughts seethed in turmoil. She was vaguely aware of high scudding clouds, and then a scattering of rain on the windscreen, blurred as Ben switched on a slow wiper to clear his vision.

The car stopped but Laurie refused to ask why.

'That's Hill Top, up there,' he said. 'Where Beatrix Potter used to live, but you can hardly see it for all the trees and the rain. 'You'll have to come back if you want to see over the house. It's very small and they only let a few people in at a time.'

'I thought you said you were in a hurry,' said Laurie after a pause.

'So I am,' he said. 'But I usually keep my promises. And I said I would show you Sawrey. Unfortunately I have no control over the weather.'

'You surprise me,' said Laurie. 'I thought you were in charge of everything around here. A little rain shouldn't cause you any problems.'

She heard a low chuckle which went straight to the centre of her very being. She dare not look at him in case that infuriating grin was there, in case it brought about that ridiculous urge to touch him. It was as if he already knew everything about her, which he didn't; as if he had some power over her, which he hadn't.

'What a little firebrand you are,' he said. 'We'd better get going before you singe the seat.'

He threw the car into gear and roared off, giving Laurie no further time to glimpse the famous seventeenth century house. There was a queue of cars for the ferry—tourists returning to their hotels and boarding houses on the eastern side of the lake. Ben reached for his brief case on the back seat and took out some papers, completely ignoring her. Once on the ferry, Laurie got out of the car and leaned on the rail, watching the water flowing below, darkly green and cool. She wondered about its depth and whether it had a monster like Loch Ness. That thought made her smile . . . it would probably look like Professor Ben Vaughan in a bad mood.

Belle Isle was a green jewel of grass amid the water, the Round House on it with its elegant white columns like some misplaced temple. It was a beautiful landmark, mystical and peaceful.

Laurie was glad when the car bumped on to firm land and nosed through the exodus. She could get a bus from Bowness or even walk from Windermere if it came to that. But Ben was driving steadily through the evening traffic of the lakeside resort and it did not seem he was going to eject her on the pavement somewhere.

He made no comment as they turned into the drive of Cumthwaite Hall, the scene of their first confrontation. As he slowed the car down in the courtyard, circling the gravel, Laurie breathed a sigh of relief. Already Cumthwaite Hall looked like home and she was longing to climb the stairs to her little flat and switch on the electric jug.

'Thank you,' she said formally. 'I did enjoy seeing Hawkshead despite the subsequent unpleasantness. I hope it didn't spoil your afternoon,' she added, with a slight emphasis on the pronoun.

She wanted to get out of the car and escape but something was holding her down. Ben's eyes were moving over every feature on her face, coming to rest on her full lips. Suddenly her mouth went dry, then as he leaned over and touched her skin she found her senses reeling into a swirling pleasure. She tried to protest but it was already too late. He was just everything she had ever wanted in a man.

As his firm mouth skimmed down to her soft lips, she began to melt in his arms, savouring the essence of him.

He tasted cool and fresh and tangy and his closeness was making her body tingle in a new and alarming way. She wanted to bury herself in the strong haven of his arms, to twist and turn, to coax and caress. Her own arms began to fasten round his muscled neck, touching his hair and the roughness of his chin.

Then suddenly she remembered his dishevelled and relaxed appearance in Priscilla's garden. Ben had come fresh from Priscilla's arms, still with her perfume on his skin, and here he was already kissing another woman, even if she was that other woman!

'That's quite enough,' she said, scrambling out of the car. 'I didn't know I was expected to pay for my ride. I suppose some consultants do extract homage due from hospital staff, but I must remind you that this is Cumthwaite Hall and not Carlisle County. I'm sorry I forgot to offer to pay you for the petrol. Would three pounds be enough? I don't know the consumption per mile of such a showy car.'

His face went pale beneath his tan and his eyes cold as granite. He looked far too dangerous for her fragile condition or composure. He reminded her of a situation she wanted to forget, reminded her that quite normal situations could esculate into real danger.

'Keep your money. And don't insult me by making such an offer again. I might be tempted to ram it down your throat.'

With a gasp of distress, Laurie ran into the hall, slamming the heavy door behind her.

CHAPTER FOUR

LAURIE tried to put Ben Vaughan right out of her mind. It was the only way when she had to concentrate on her work. Several students had neck and spine problems that she felt stemmed from emotional difficulties and they needed special individual treatment. This kind of challenge took all her energy and thought.

If she found herself thinking of him, then she dismissed those thoughts abruptly. Her cheeks burned when she remembered the way he had spoken to her; then the way he had kissed her and her wanton response. He was nothing but a low opportunist like a lot of men, despite his serious and responsible work.

Laurie knew there were immense problems with the misuse and side-effects of prescribed drugs which the medical profession had not realised at first in the euphoria of new discoveries by the drug companies. Thalidomide was only one of the villains, perhaps the most publicised because of its tragic consequences. Now there were the Opren sufferers. Professor Vaughan had quite a task educating his contemporaries.

That was one reason why many people were becoming interested in homeopathy—there were no side-effects and patients never died from the treatment. Faith was studying the use of homeopathic remedies though no one looked less like a medieval herb woman, with her elegant grey-streaked hair and casual but expensive clothes.

'We concentrate on treating the patient as a whole rather than the disease,' she told Laurie. 'Our remedies stimulate the body's natural power of recovery.'

'I can remember my mother having a bottle of arnica in her medicine cupboard,' said Laurie.

'She was very wise. It's a fall herb, wonderful for bruising. And that's not all it can do. We've some here if you ever trip over a rock!'

'How reassuring,' Laurie laughed. 'But I doubt if I'll go rock-climbing. I've not much head for heights and I know nothing about mountaineering.'

'You must come fell walking with James and me. We love to get away in the hills. The views in Cumbria are superb. You would enjoy it.'

'Thanks, I will . . . someday, if I won't be in the way.'

'Nonsense,' said Faith, brushing some fluff off her pleated skirt. 'You'd be welcome.'

Laurie felt a twinge of loneliness. How predictably everyone paired up. Faith and James, Ben and Priscilla, Tasmin had a steady boyfriend who worked in a Windermere hotel and Melanie was particularly keen on a young man who had damaged his knee in a riding accident and came for private tuition. There was probably even a Mr Olive somewhere, breakfastless but still half of a couple. That left Bruce for Laurie and she did not particularly want him.

She scolded herself for being pessimistic. What did it matter these days? She could be single and happy if her career was satisfying. In fact that kind of future could be very pleasant, undemanding and peaceful. Some women chose to be single rather than get married just for the sake of a wedding ring and a husband.

'I'd like to stay here forever,' said Laurie, leaning back in the sunshine. They were sitting on the stone steps that led from the house down to the parkland. It was the mid-morning break when tea and coffee were served and a selection of herbal teas. There were apples and Kendal biscuits for those whose appetites had been rekindled by the morning's work.

'Wouldn't we all?' said Melanie. 'But it all depends on Mr High and Mighty. The lease of Cumthwaite Hall is up this year and if it isn't renewed where will the School go then? We can hardly teach without a roof over our heads.'

'Not in this climate,' said Tasmin.

Laurie's heart fell. Just when she thought there was some stability coming into her life. She felt so at home living at the Hall, so secure in her turret flat with her bits and pieces unpacked and around her. Surely whoever owned Cumthwaite Hall wouldn't make the school close when it was doing such good work?

'Why won't the owner renew the lease?' Laurie heard herself asking in a careful voice.

'Well, we don't know for sure yet, but there are rumours that some hotel group is after the property. You must admit it would make a marvellous hotel, right on the edge of the lake with all this lovely old stone and mullioned windows.'

'But is it large enough for a hotel?'

'Perhaps they're thinking of making it into a small country club with a few suites of luxury accommodation. People with money don't always want big hotels. It's comfort, service and privacy that they want. Particularly privacy. Pop stars and business tycoons—they want to be protected from the eye of the media.'

'It's a pity they don't want to learn the Alexander Technique,' said Laurie. 'All that bad posture at Board Meetings can't be good for anyone.'

'Stockbrokers' hunch,'

'Bankers' bump.'

'Millionaires' slouch.'

'All in need of a little basic semi-supine!' They laughed and the good-humour of the group was self-healing in itself. They could hear distant music and the swish of the lake steamers on the water. The lake was packed with water traffic, boats, yachts and luxury launches churning up and down all day in every direction, from Lakeside to Waterhead. It was like an aquatic Trafalgar Square in the rush hour.

Faith looked up with concern. 'There's going to be an accident one day. All those steamers, crowded with people. And some of the public have never handled a small boat before. It's a terrible hazard. No traffic controller in charge of that lot.'

Tasmin nodded. 'It would be awful. Let's not think about anything happening. We don't want to spoil such a lovely morning.'

'I think I'll go down to the lake just for a few minutes. I can't keep away from the water. It has a hypnotic affect on me,' said Laurie, standing up.

Melanie giggled. 'Fascinating how these Londoners get hooked on Windermere. Wonder what else Laurie will get hooked on?'

'Or on whom?'

'How about Mr High and Mighty?'

'No, he's only interested in his career.'

'Laurie could sacrifice herself for the sake of the school.'

'What better cause!' they teased.

'Not me, count me out,' said Laurie, brushing her spiky fringe from her eyes. 'Not even as a sacrifice. I intend to remain heart free.'

She ran down the grass, the breeze loosened her long hair from its floppy bow. She had bought two silky track suits to work in, one lilac and white and the other coral and white. They made her look like a spring flower, fresh and delicate. They were such a contrast to her stiff and unflattering nurse's uniform, she felt perpetually on holiday, hardly like working at all.

No one was going to spoil things for her here, she resolved as she walked along the water's edge. She did not want another Bruce. She climbed over a low stone wall and sat on it, admiring the view of man and nature existing side by side in harmony. But it would not take long to leave the commercialism of the resorts behind and be alone in the stillness of the fells. There were broad routes to the peaks, but also secret paths and hidden tracks. One day she would seek them out.

'Hey you! Don't you realise this is private property? I should have thought with 123 acres to roam in, you could manage to keep off my half-acre of shore.'

Ben Vaughan was coming out of the lake, water streaming off his brown hairy chest, muscles gleaming in the sunlight. He ran a hand over his face, pushing the wet hair back. He wasn't wearing swimming trunks, but instead a pair of cut-off jeans clung wetly to his thighs.

'Sorry,' said Laurie, looking away from his glistening body. She had no intention of being reminded of the intimacy of their parting. 'I didn't know that any of the grounds were private. I thought it all went with Cumthwaite Hall.'

'I live in the Boathouse and the walled area is private,' he said, bounding up the shore, shaking water everywhere. 'I find it necessary to make the boundary quite clear. I don't want your guests or students, whatever you call them, tramping all over the place.'

'We're all far too occupied for tramping,' said Laurie, slipping off the wall. 'Sorry to have disturbed your swim.'

'I wasn't swimming for pleasure. My boat's broken down. I've come ashore for some parts.'

Laurie looked across the lake. A small sleek white cruiser bobbed at anchor some two hundred yards out, sun glinting on the cabin windows and varnished deck.

'Is that your boat?'

'Yes. She had a nice clean line, hasn't she?'

'Doctoring must pay well,' Laurie could not resist saying. 'A Mercedes and a boat.'

He shot her a hostile glance. 'Lecturing pays well. Anything else you want to know? You believe in saying what you think.'

There was a small, startled silence but Laurie was not one to resist a challenge. 'Do you know what nurses earn?' she said. 'They're lucky if there's enough over at the end of the week to buy a new pair of tights, let alone a cabin cruiser.'

'I will ignore your usual exaggeration of the facts. I agree that nurses are poorly paid. What do you want me to do about it? Take on the NHS single-handed? Hand my salary back? What would you do?'

'Fight—fight for equality.'

'Okay. The first nurse who can deliver my lecture on Cephalosporins can have my salary. Is that fair? You'll know, of course, that the principle side effect is hypersensitivity and also severe bleeding, particularly in elderly or debilitated patients.'

'That's not fair,' Laurie raged. 'No nurse has had the opportunity of your experience or your research.'

'Which is what I'm paid for, miss,' he said with a decisive nod, putting an end to the argument.

The whole of Laurie's professional career had been based on practical work; she was not used to waging a war of words, even though at times she had a blistering tongue. But her new life was important and she believed in its disciplines implicitly.

'Research is important for the Alexander Technique too,' she said, being careful not to sound bossy. 'If you are interested I can show you photographic evidence produced by Frank Jones using multiple-image photography and a strain-gauge platform. Or you could yourself do a simple measurement test showing the expansion of fluid in the intervertebral discs after fifteen minutes of the semi-supine.'

'More long words. My, what a lot jargon they have pumped into you.'

'Look out!' Laurie shrieked. 'Stop!'

Ben immediately responded with the normal startle pattern, his chest and knees tensed, his shoulders rose, jaw clenched. Laurie put her hands on his neck so that he could not move. It was gentle but firm touch, holding his position in place.

'Think about how your body feels at this moment,' she said in a pleasant matter of fact way. 'It takes a little thought because we are not used to analysing how we are. Can you feel the tension in your neck? Look at your raised shoulders. What's happened to your breathing?'

'That was a trick,' Ben gasped, astonished.

'I wanted to show the typical response to fear. It's instinctive and quite normal. But it also demonstrates the difference between an abnormal head-neck-torso position and a balanced resting state.'

'I don't believe this,' he said.

'Come on, be honest. Kids can do better than this. Think how your neck feels. There's tension in the muscles, isn't there, just here?'

'If you say so.'

Laurie kept her patience with difficulty. She knew he was deliberately not co-operating. She had used the startle pattern many times as a demonstration and it always worked. She used it on herself too when she needed a quick reminder of use and misuse.

'Let's think about your jaw instead,' she said, putting the slightest pressure on the clenched muscles. She saw a small nerve flicker in his cheek. She was far closer than she intended to be and he was amused by her sudden awareness.

'Yes, teacher,' he said affably. 'That was nice, that little stroking thing. Could you do it again? No wonder you give private lessons.'

Laurie stood back on her heels, dropping her hands. 'There is nothing physical about a teacher's touch. It is purely guidance, to give a student the experience of balanced use.'

'Ah,' he said, nodding wisely, pretending to understand every word. 'What wonderful work you do.'

Laurie's hazel eyes glittered. 'I'm not wasting any more time on you,' she said. 'You obviously intend to make fun of everything I say and do. Fortunately there are plenty of people with open minds, interested and willing to learn a better way of using their bodies. Look at yourself. Someone, sometime, obviously said you were too tall, so you hunch your shoulders to compensate, storing up all sorts of problems for the future.'

She turned to leave.

'Where are you going?'

'Back to the Hall. Classes start again soon.'

'How incredibly boring.'

'Quite the contrary, Professor Vaughan. They are incredibly exciting. We have for ages been padding ourselves with upholstery and central heating; it's a revelation to get in touch with our natural mechanism.' She knew it sounded pompous and prim but he brought out the worst in her.

He looked at her with mock alarm. 'I don't think I've lost touch with my natural mechanism.'

Laurie ignored the crude remark, a relic of his medical student days, she supposed. 'It might interest you to know that we lose the ability to organise our bodies at about eight years old. A child that has been allowed to sit up and stand in its own chosen time will move easily and beautifully. But then the tensions and strains of the family and school begin misuse and the practise of posture-swopping is adopted.'

He looked at his watch impatiently. 'I'm not in the market for conversion, Miss Young. Your particular cult doesn't interest me in the slightest. I think I'm the only qualified lecturer present and at least mine are based on statistics and research and not lifted straight from a textbook.'

'Oh!' For a moment Laurie was lost for words. Her eyes went flinty green, their softness vanishing in a spurt of anger. 'You're making snap judgements on a technique you know absolutely nothing about.'

'I know your technique is like trying to fix a broken leg with sticking plaster.'

'That's it!' Laurie fumed. 'You are so pompous. I've never met anyone quite so full of himself. You've no time for alternative medicines, have you? Other thoughts, opinions, beliefs, are arbitrary dismissed simply because they don't coincide with yours. I'm not suprised you've become a lecturer. It suits you standing up there on a platform, spouting away, no one daring to interrupt you. Your word taken as law. That's not real medicine, you know. Real medicine is on the wards and in the operating theatres, curing people, amongst all the blood and guts.'

'I had thought my work was about preventing death and suffering,' he said coldly.

'Work?' Laurie rapped. It was as if her hundreds of hours of overtime, night duty, panics and crises were suddenly crushed into the ground by some ruthless demolition machine. 'You don't know the meaning of the word. If you think swanning around the country in a chaffeur-driven car is work, then boy, you need a sharp lesson on what really goes on in this world. Just how many of your patients can spend their mornings messing about in boats? Or their afternoons visiting famous artists? I suggest you wipe the water out of your eyes, Professor Vaughan and take a long look at real life, then perhaps you might have a little humanity.'

Laurie turned on her heel, flushed and furious. She was fighting to calm down, baffled that he of all people should make her lose control of herself. He was the demolition machine! He managed to irritate and infuriate her every time they met. There had to be an end to it. She must simply keep right out of his way, however difficult or awkward that might be.

She ran into the big billiards room which had been converted for the practical work. Melanie and Tasmin were already laying out the rugs on the floor and setting up the two treatment tables. Laurie went to the cupboard to get piles of old Reader's Digests.

'Sorry I'm late,' she said hurriedly. 'I've just had the most awful row with that pompous professor down at the Boathouse. He really is so arrogant and stupid, I couldn't help it. I didn't mean to get angry but he was so snide about what we are doing here, I just let fly.'

Melanie pretended a look of shock and horror. 'Heavens, don't tell James. He won't be pleased. We are always supposed to try and avoid getting into arguments about the Alexander Technique.'

'And the dishy doctor is the last person to cross words with,' said Tasmin.

'Well, it was his fault. He was so high-handed and rude to me. Who does he think he is, anyway?' Laurie was beginning to recover from the encounter as the pleasant atmosphere of the school calmed her frayed nerves.

'Who is he?' said Tasmin, locking the legs of the padded table. 'Well, just about the most important person for the continuation of this School. You've just named him. Mr High and Mighty himself. He holds the future of Cumthwaite Hall in his hands.'

Laurie's face went pale. 'You don't mean . . .? Mr High and Mighty? You were talking this morning about the lease of Cumthwaite Hall, that it might not be renewed . . .'

'Ben Vaughan owns Cumthwaite Hall. He used to live here when he was a boy. It was the family home for several generations. Then his parents died and the Hall was empty for quite a while. He let James have it at a very reasonable rent, but now the lease is up and it may not be renewed. You can't blame him, if he's had a better offer.'

'But he was so critical of the Alexander Technique. I told him he didn't know the m-meaning of real work,' Laurie faltered.

'That was really tactful. The man holds down two jobs. He works night shifts at Carlisle County so that he's free to lecture during the day.' Tasmin gave her a compassionate smile. 'You've put your foot in it, up to the ankle.'

The dawning comprehension of what she had done filled Laurie with icy dismay. She had upset the one person who could close the school. And she had known about his involvement with the Carlisle County. Olive had told her the first morning. But she had been so tired from the overnight drive, she had assumed it was lecturing.

A long sigh left her lips—she was shattered. Tears stung her eyes when she thought of the awful things she had said to him. The newest member of staff and she had probably ruined everything for everyone, the school and the students. It would have been better for them if she had never come to Cumthwaite Hall, and if she had never met Ben Vaughan.

'Why aren't you angry with me?' said Laurie, aghast.

'What good would it do?' said Tasmin calmly.

'It wouldn't undo what has already been said,' Melanie put in.

Laurie shivered as if the ghost of a long-gone nun had brushed by, the hem of her habit causing a chilly draught.

'Cold, dear?' said Milly Washbourne, her next student for individual tuition. 'It's coming in out of the sun that does it. This room is so cool with the high ceilings.'

'Perhaps it was a ghost,' said Laurie ruefully.

Milly Washbourne was their oldest student that week, a grey-haired retired teacher who was determined to improve the years ahead. It was never too late to learn, and she was keen to absorb everything in her week at Cumthwaite Hall. So she was striving, trying too hard to correct a lifetime of misuse in one week.

Laurie moved her gently into the right position, trying to free the habitually held cramped head and shoulder position of a teacher writing on a blackboard.

'Don't think in terms of doing,' said Laurie quietly, lifting Milly's arm loosely. 'Let me do everything.'

As she worked on Milly, Laurie concentrated on her ability to convey to the weary muscles the correct amount of tension necessary with manual guidance.

'I always feel I'm doing the wrong thing.' Milly murmured, her eyes closed.

'Don't be anxious,' said Laurie patiently. 'It will come in time. Don't do anything.'

By lunch time, Laurie was worn out. It did take a lot of energy. Sometimes she felt she was floating on fatigue. But this morning, it had been worse. She had wasted energy arguing with Ben, then the remorse had sapped her strength still further. She knew what she had to do.

The school broke up . . . some students went out to eat, some on sight-seeing trips around Windermere, some to meditate and think about what they had learnt that morning. Other students took text books, notepads, sketching paper, under the scattered and shady trees of the grounds, at liberty now to spend the afternoon as they wished.

Laurie went straight to her flat and changed out of the working track suit. She put on a low-backed navy swimsuit and pottered about, searching for what she needed. There was only one way to dress for the coming interview and that was sackcloth and ashes.

She slipped unseen out of the Hall and across the parkland. It would be ridiculous to have got her courage together just to find that he had gone out. But she saw the gleam of his parked Mercedes through the leaves and was reassured that at least she could get this over quickly.

Her hand fluttered to her throat. She wondered if she was strong enough physically or emotionally to do what she was going to do. But for the sake of her new friends, she must not back out. She had never lacked courage—only that once, that unforgettable, loathsome Saturday, for which she had never forgiven herself.

She began climbing over the dry stone wall. It was not easy. It seemed to have got higher since that morning and her knees were like jelly.

Hold on, Laurie, she told herself. He isn't an ogre, even if he acts like one. He can't eat you. He'll make you feel small, maybe but that would save on dieting . . .

But she was not in the mood for joking. Her mission was far too serious. She hoped she would find the right words when the time came, but if she was thrown by his attitude then she would be tongue-tied to the point of silence.

Laurie was so deep in thought she did not see him until it was almost too late. He was stretched out on a grassy bank, sound asleep, dark head cradled on a bent arm. In sleep, the hardness of his jaw was softened and the lashes of his steely eyes fanned childishly on his tanned cheeks.

Even as she took in those new disturbing aspects of his looks, her toe caught in something and she found herself flying through the air, arms outstretched, an exclamation on her lips. She landed half on top of him, sprawled in an ungainly manner, legs tangled with his, her face against his bare shoulder.

He jolted awake, struggling to sit up, instinctively grabbing her arms as if ready to fight off some wild beast. He took one look at her startled face and flopped back, groaning.

'Oh no, not you. I don't believe it. What are you trying to do? Persecute me? Why not just make a little doll and stick pins in when you've a minute to spare.'

Laurie pushed herself up, straightening her untidy hair. She could not bear to look at him. All her traitorous senses were reeling from the hard feel of his body as she lay on him, the warmth of his bare flesh and the tangy smell of his skin. She savoured all the details, imprinting them on her mind just as the contours of his body were still imprinted on her skin. If only everything had been different, she could obliterate the inches between them with a sweet smile—but it was more than any measurable distance, they were worlds apart.

'Not talking?' he remarked. 'Well, that makes a change. At least, I shan't get another lecture. Have you perhaps decided on physical attacks this afternoon, making sure that I'm asleep first. Surprise does always have an advantage.'

Laurie shut her ears to his mocking voice even though the words were unfair. She had come here for a purpose and it would not help if she immediately got into another argument with him.

'I fell over the strap of your binoculars which were lying here unattended,' she said, untangling her foot.

'Yes, I usually let them look after themselves,' he

growled. 'They are quite trustworthy.'

She could not see the expression in his eyes as his lids were still closed, but he was obviously baiting her. She resisted all her natural urge to answer back. Many years ago her sister tutor had warned her, 'That tongue of yours will bite back one day, Nurse Young . . .'

Was she discovering her true self at this lakeland paradise, perhaps? The idea was fragile, fleeting, almost a reassessment of her purpose in life. Restlessly she wanted to get away, to think about these new aspects, yet she could not move. She seemed chained to the ground, like Gulliver, with invisible bonds. There was some tenuous link between her and this truck driver cum professor, the man lying on his back quite oblivious to her, his broad chest rising and falling with regular breathing. But what it was about him was a mystery. Nor did she know if she even cared. He was an elusive mixture of sophistication and toughness, in layers that surfaced alternately with tantilising swiftness.

'I daresay you'll recognise me if you see me again,' he said, his eyes flying open to catch her close scrutiny.

Laurie shifted back and sat on her heels. She tried to let go of all the feelings of tightness, to loosen her muscles, to be well balanced in that position.

'Is this a demonstration of the semi-supine?' he asked.

'No, it isn't,' she said.

'May I ask what you are doing here? As I think I explained to you this morning, this is my private shore and I do like to enjoy the odd nap undisturbed and unmolested.'

Laurie took a deep breath. She tried to make her voice mundane and ordinary. 'You may have noticed what I am wearing,' she began, smoothing her hips.

His mouth twitched as he calculated his reply. 'Yes,' he said slowly. 'I had noticed. I was too polite to mention it, of course. Is it a new fashion?'

'It's sackcloth and ashes,' said Laurie.

'Ah . . .' he nodded. 'And I thought it was a couple of dustbin liners.'

'It was the nearest I could get.'

'Very enterprising.'

'I've come to apologise for . . . for my behaviour this morning. I spoke without thinking.' Laurie felt painfully gauche and her apology did not ring true. She tried to instil more sincerity into her voice though it was a struggle. 'I did not mean half of what I said.'

'But you did mean the other half?'

'I got carried away. And I was under stress.' She was remembering how thoroughly he had once kissed her. 'And that wasn't fair,' she added without thinking.

'I beg your pardon? I didn't quite catch that. This is all such a lovely novelty, I don't want to miss a word.'

'I mean, I wasn't fair. I didn't realise that you had been working all night at the hospital, and now I've spoilt your afternoon sleep. I'd better clear off and let you catch up. Only I do hope you'll forgive me and perhaps try to forget the silly things I said.' She kept her eyes demurely down.

He balanced his chin on the palm of his hand. She was quite luminously beautiful, like a young girl, all confusion and innocence. Her mouth was cherry pink, softly curving and gentle, without any sticky lipstick. He wanted to kiss her very much and he did not really know why.

'There's no need to go,' he said. 'I like this apology business. How about a little more? What else did you say to me that was very rude?'

'I said you were p-pompous.'

'Oh yes, so you did. Pompous. Now that really hurt my pride. I shall require an especially abject apology for such an insult.'

She stared at the brown hollow in his throat beneath his

firm jutting chin, feeling utterly transparent. He was teasing her, some of the gauntness leaving his face as he relaxed. Her heart full, she gave him a small, brief smile.

'I'm not particularly good at abject apologies, it's ordinary run-of-the-mill ones I'm usually having to make,' said Laurie, folding her hands in her lap.

She turned away to watch the water of the lake, ruffled by a breeze, lapping the shore with little noises. The rearing ridges of mountain behind mountain were reflected in the purity of the lake like the backcloth of a vast theatre. The occasional bleating of sheep came echoing down from the fells. It was so different from the city life, so clean and fresh and endlessly peaceful. Blocks of flats and offices might come and go, but these mountains were awesomely ancient, crags and gullies thrown up by earthquakes millions of years ago.

He unwound his long shape and stood up. Her shoulders were set in sadness and he wondered what had changed her mood. He had a lot to do but he did not want to leave her too abruptly. She looked vulnerable; despite her sharp tongue, he was aware that she could easily be hurt.

'Well, shall we say that all is forgiven and we'll forget the whole incident. I daresay I've said a few things I now regret. You're quite a little devil when you're roused.' He began to gather up his things from the bank. Laurie handed him the binoculars.

'Thanks. And thank you for coming in sackcloth and ashes,' he added. 'I appreciate the gesture. You could take them off now. That plastic must be very uncomfortable to wear.'

'It's horrid. Hot and sticky.'

She struggled to get out of the bin bags and Ben knelt down, hiding his laughter, to help her get divested. The black plastic was stuck in places to her skin and he had to ease if off gently.

'This is like peeling a ripe banana,' he chuckled, his
fingers sliding over her damp skin. For a second his hand
trembled as it poised over the seductive curve of her bare
thigh. Laurie's eyes flared with alarm, her skin tingling at
his touch. The whole magnificent outline of his shoulders
blocked out the sky and it was as if the world was made
entirely of him.

She emerged from the plastic, hot and dishevelled, her
trim navy swimsuit dark with perspiration. His eyes
relished the soft swell of her bosom and the shadowy cleft
that promised such tantalising sweetness. He leaned
forward and pushed back her hair, his fingers brushing
the lobe of her ear. She caught her breath with a sense of
pleasure and turned, without thinking, towards him.

'I think you had better go,' he said roughly, thrusting
his hands into the belt of his jeans. 'I might gobble a little
girl like you for tea. Why don't you go for a swim and
cool off?'

'Are you coming with me?' she asked.

'Do you want me to?'

'It would be friendly. Since we have made a truce.'

His eyes were teasing. 'Friendly, is that what we are
now? I think I might get to like that.'

He began to look at her, his eyes clouding as they
travelled over her gentle curves and the slender length of
her thighs and legs. Laurie felt her heart begin to race and
she knew she had to get away.

'Don't be alarmed,' he said huskily. 'I don't often have
such a beautiful body to look at. The bodies I see are
usually ill or damaged, or worse still, dead.' His fingers
traces the line of her shoulder down to the small indent of
her elbow, which he stroked with a kind of curiosity. 'I
had forgotten how beautiful and soft a woman can be.
Your skin it's so luminous . . . like moonsilk.'

Laurie became aware of her breasts, how they were tightening and swelling against her swimsuit, how she was swaying towards him silently pleading for his hands to move to more intimate places. Her mind tried to resist the craving that was reducing her body to no more than a primeval creature; if only the inhibitions of civilisation could be stripped aside and she could let Ben carry her away to his cave.

He slipped off the shoulder straps of her swimsuit, his mouth beginning an exploration of her neck and the soft hollow of her throat, his hands steadying her hips against him in case she fell. An exquisite sensation shot through her limbs, bringing her immediately quiveringly to her senses.

Laurie recoiled from him. She ached to say words that were smart and sophisticated, but none came into her head. Instead she stuttered something stupid about the beach being his private property.

'The lake isn't private,' he said harshly.

'Is it safe?'

'Safer than on shore,' he said. He ran into the water and dived through the waves, surfacing far out and beginning a powerful crawl towards his boat. She followed him slowly, glad when the cool water crossed over her heated body and brought her back to some kind of sanity.

CHAPTER FIVE

THE NEXT time Laurie was in Bowness she remembered to buy herself a few bits and pieces for the flat. She brought some bone china mugs, a crystal vase and a couple of scatter cushions to add her own touches to the room. She loved flowers but finding a florists was not easy. There were so many souvenir shops bulging with objects decorated with views of Windermere. Although she was not hungry she could not resist some locally made ice-cream. The length of the queue was an indication of its popularity, and Laurie was happy to stand in line for a large, luscious peach-flavoured cornet.

The lakeside resort was busy and bustling, thronged with holidaymakers making their way to the point of embarkation for the steamers and other smaller boats at the jetties. Several big white hotels stood sentinel on the shores, making the necessary preparations to absorb the folk back for evening meals. Laurie had never realised that the tourist trade was so thriving in the Lake District. It was all good for business, as long as it did not spoil the rural beauty of the area.

She licked at the fast melting ice-cream. It became a race against time as the peachy cream began to run down the biscuit cone and then dribble down her wrist. She could not help grinning at herself. No one had ever seen Sister Young behaving so outrageously in public, but then she was plain Miss Young now and plain Miss Young could do what she liked.

Now she needed something to wipe her fingers on. She went into a fairly large chemists and bought a packet of moist tissues. As Laurie was leaving she became aware of a commotion by the door and a gathering of people. She moved closer, curious and with a tinge of apprehension. It always gave her a nervous gut feeling when being confronted by the unknown.

An elderly woman was on the pavement, sprawled half in and half out of the doorway. She was not moving. Her handbag had fallen open and its contents were rolling in all directions. Laurie took in the situation at a glance.

'Excuse me, please,' she said. 'Out of the way, please. Let me through.'

No one moved and Laurie had to push her way through the crowd. People were so unhelpful at an accident; they just wanted to stand and gawp.

'Give the woman air. She needs air. Please let me get to her,' she said urgently. 'And stand back.'

Laurie went down on her knees by the woman. She seemed to have fainted. Laurie turned her over so that the woman was flat on her back, immediately recognising the crinkled grey hair and pale, clammy face.

'Why Miss Washbourne. Miss Washbourne! It's Laurie Young here. Can you hear me?'

Milly Washbourne was breathing rapidly and Laurie quickly unfastened the button at the neck of her blouse and the waistband of her skirt. She carefully moved the elderly woman into the shade of the doorway and looked round for an assistant or someone with an honest face.

'Can you pick up the lady's things?' she asked a young girl with a fair pony-tail. 'They are all over the place. It would be awful if she lost her money and her keys.'

'Okay,' said the schoolgirl, scrabbling around the pavement.

A shop assistant came over, bustling and inquisitive. 'What's going on? Keep the doorway clear, please. Is the lady all right?'

'I think she's just fainted,' said Laurie. 'But do you have a first aid department, or a first aider around?'

'No, I'm sorry. This is just a shop.'

'But it is a chemist's shop!'

'Sorry, we only sell things.'

'Well, that's ridiculous. Perhaps you could at least call an ambulance. This lady ought to be seen at a hospital.' Laurie was checking Milly's pulse. It was feeble and her breathing was irregular, her pupils dilated. Laurie was worried. 'I must get her to a hospital.'

The assistant looked helpless. 'An ambulance?'

'Yes, one of those moving vehicles on four wheels. Part of the emergency service,' Laurie snapped, her temper rising.

Milly Washbourne stirred and her eye-lids fluttered. She moaned slightly. Laurie fanned the air around her.

'Hello, Milly . . . are you all right? Can you hear me?'

'Oh . . . Laurie?' Milly Washbourne breathed, her sparse lashes fluttering. 'Whatever happened?'

'I think you fainted. Don't worry. How are you feeling now?'

'How stupid of me,' said Milly. 'I feel perfectly all right. 'I'd better get home.'

Laurie lifted Milly into a sitting position, supporting her. 'I think I ought to get you to a hospital, just for a check up, to be on the safe side.'

'Nonsense. I can't go to hospital. There are my cats to look after. Who would feed them? I've got to get home. Just help me get to my feet. Where's my bag? Thank you, my dear.'

The manager of the shop appeared, bringing a chair, and they helped Miss Washbourne onto it. The manager was at pains to explain to Laurie that the shop did not feel responsible for the lady's faint as she had not been in their shop, was not a customer and had in fact been on the pavement when she fainted.

'For heaven's sake,' said Laurie. 'Relax. No one is taking you to court. I only asked if you could ring for an ambulance. What a fuss.'

Milly Washbourne was adamant about going straight home. There was no persuading her without a scene. She allowed Laurie to call a taxi and accompany her, but insisted on paying the fare herself. She lived on the outskirts of Windermere in an old stone cottage with three gorgeous long-haired cats who came to meet her, fluffy tails held in the air in greeting.

'Hello my darlings,' she called. 'Have you missed me?' They purred round her ankles, insisting that they had.

Laurie took Milly indoors and settled her in an armchair, went through into the tiny old-fashioned stone-flagged kitchen and made a pot of tea. The cats were milling about, maiowing and getting in the way, obviously convinced their suppertime came first.

'You can all wait a few minutes,' said Laurie pushing an insistent furry head away. 'You look well fed.'

'I really enjoyed my week at Cumthwaite Hall,' said Milly who seemed to have recovered from her faint. 'And I'm still doing my semi-supine every day.'

'You ought to come back for a private lesson every week,' said Laurie, stroking the big ginger tom who was acting as spokescat for the other two. 'It would really help.'

'I'd like to, my dear, but I can't afford it. I only have my pension. That week was a little treat.' She caught Laurie's expression of concern. 'But it was worth every penny. You were all so kind to an old woman like me.'

'You're not an old woman. People are people,' said Laurie. 'Age has nothing to do with what people are like and how they are. You have a back like everyone else, and that's how we see you.'

'How refreshing,' said Milly, putting down her cup.

'Now I'd better feed my cats. They'll be thinking I've forsaken them soon.'

'I'll do it,' said Laurie. 'You sit still. Just tell me which tin to open.'

'A tin of pink salmon, dear, and you'll be their friend for life.'

Laurie had to catch two different buses to get back to Cumthwaite Hall and it was getting quite dark when the second one dropped her at the end of the lane to walk the last half-mile. It was not an easy journey, but Milly had managed to do it twice a day to and from the course. On the bus Laurie discovered that someone had lifted the packet of tissues from her shopping bag. So much for being a Good Samaritan.

She thought a lot about Milly Washbourne's loss of consciousness. She did not think it was simply the heat. Milly ought to see a doctor but how could she persuade a stubborn old lady to do that?

The lane was cool and creepy with so many overhanging trees, the wind rustling in the leaves as if an army of small creatures was secretly following her. She would be glad when her small car was back on the road. She heard a car coming along the lane, and stepped into the undergrowth to let it go by.

'Oh no,' she groaned under her breath, as the metallic Mercedes drew to a stop and Ben wound down a window.

'Hello, Laurie. No wheels? Like a lift?'

'No, thank you. It's not far to walk.'

'Don't argue. It'll be dark soon. Get in.'

'If you say so.' Laurie got into his car, sinking back on to the wide upholstered seat. She stifled a yawn, letting her body accept the weariness that was creeping over her. It had been a busy day and she had been on her feet most of it.

'Tired?' he asked.

'Yes. The . . . my kind of work . . .' she chose her words carefully. It was like treading on glass. She was not going to get into an argument with him. 'Takes a lot of physical energy and concentration.'

'So I should imagine,' he replied, also being careful.

'What about you?'

'I've been lecturing to a group of Manchester based hospitals . . . spouting, as you so aptly put it. I was talking about beta-blockers. You may have heard of them.'

'Athletes and musicians,' said Laurie with feigned innocence. She still had no intention of letting him find out she was a trained nurse. 'It alleviates stage fright. Stops hands trembling and knees knocking.'

'Yes, their use has spread but they were originally developed for heart and vascular conditions. We don't know an awful lot about them as yet.'

Ben turned into the drive and the long avenue of trees ahead was quiet and peaceful. Laurie felt her head nodding as the warmth and comfort of the car invaded her body. And the engine purr was low and powerful, like a lullaby. Had she eaten? She could hardly remember that far back. Nothing except that delicious ice cream and a cup of tea with Milly. She wished they could just drive on forever, anywhere, it wouldn't matter.

'Do you feel like driving to John O'Groats?' she murmured drowsily.

'Not at this particular moment. Is that where you want to go?'

'I just thought that if you did, then I wouldn't have to get out of the car.'

Ben chuckled quietly and lifted his foot off the accelerator so that the car slowed down to a crawl.

'If I'd known you were that keen on my company,' he remarked. 'I would have put in a little detour round the lake.'

Laurie was wide awake in an instant as if he had actually touched her. It was the teasing, intimate tone of his voice that sharpened her defences. Even the thought of several hours in his company was unnerving. What an odd reaction, she thought, when she did not really like him. Oh yes, she could appreciate his good looks and his splendid masculine body, as one could admire a striking or powerful portrait.

He had a vital, harnessed strength that was magnetic, that she unconsciously wanted, that she needed. There had never been a strong man in her life, never a man to support or take care of her. She did not remember her parents. They had parted when she was small and for some reason she had gone to live with an aunt, a kind but overworked woman who tried to give her niece a home. No one had ever bothered to fully explain it to her. She knew her father had been a serving Marine and her mother had returned to live in her native Norway. Perhaps they thought the transition to a different country and different language would have been too difficult for a child.

Since leaving school, she had been on her own, had to stand on her own two feet. Nothing had been easy. Her heart was pounding as she smoothed her skirt over her knees.

'Can I ask you something?' she said.

'Fire ahead.'

'I know it's none of my business, but one of our older students, a really lovely lady, isn't too well. I think she ought to see a doctor. She has a feeble pulse and she might have some heart problem. I've suggested that she should go to her doctor but she won't listen to me. She's pretty stubborn and is more concerned about feeding her cats than looking after herself.'

It was a long speech for Laurie, but she felt strongly that Milly Washbourne should have medical attention. She was not sure what she ought to do, but hoped Ben would advise her.

'May I ask how you came to make a diagnosis of this lady's condition?'

Laurie knew straight away that she had made a big mistake, his voice had lost all its former warmth and was as cold as steel. She took another deep breath and tried to explain.

'Well, I was shopping in Bowness today and this lady, Milly Washbourne, fainted in a shop, er . . . outside a shop actually. I helped to look after her . . .'

'And you know all about heart problems, do you? Part of your training for the Alexander Technique? How very clever of you. You recognise all the signs, do you? Perhaps you'd like to tell me what they are,' Ben said bluntly.

'No, of course, it's not part of the training—'

'As a dedicated teacher, surely you should be insisting that your technique has the answer? Or is it that when things get serious, you feel that conventional medicine has a place in the scheme of things?'

'Oh dear,' Laurie moaned. 'Now you're annoyed with me again.'

'Of course, I'm annoyed at your presumption. You learn a bit about breathing and relaxation and how to stand up straight. You wear a pretty track suit, play at teaching classes and think you're qualified to know everything. You really take the cake. A little bit of knowledge can be dangerous.'

'I'm concerned about my friend,' Laurie said between her teeth. 'And I'd like your advice.'

'This is so touching,' said Ben. 'I suppose I should be flattered—on the other hand I don't need you to tell me my responsibilities. What am I supposed to do? Pay a casual visit and force your ailing friend into seeing a doctor? And probably scare the daylights out of her at the same time. Why don't you stop meddling in concerns you know nothing about? Stick to your semi-supine and leave real medicine to the professionals.'

Laurie felt her anger rising. His cool withdrawl and demolition of her good intentions was humiliating—unforgiveable. She was torn between fury at his cruelty and a helpless yearning for a return to those earlier moments of pleasant intimacy and friendly teasing. He had certainly cooled off faster than a dip in the lake in winter.

'I'm sorry I asked you,' she said. 'I might have known it's impossible for you to act like a normal human being. Perhaps James will know someone more approachable and sympathetic. God knows, that's all I wanted . . . someone to listen and advise. It was a big mistake to ask you. Thanks for nothing.'

'Surely this is an opportunity to prove that the Alexander Technique can help your elderly friend? How about arranging some demonstrations for me?'

Laurie sighed. 'You know that's impossible.'

'Why not, you're so keen to enlist my approbation and approval. I suppose my name would make an excellent addition to the school's prospectus.'

'What a ridiculous suggestion. The school doesn't need your name or anyone's else's to enhance its reputation. People come to us from all over the world. We don't advertise. It's all by word of mouth.'

'You must be their best advertisement, all that pioneering zeal and enthusiasm. And there may even be a tender heart beneath that spitfire exterior.'

Laurie avoided looking at him. She knew she would be torn between her strong attraction to him, and her disappointment in his attitude. 'That's something you're never likely to find out,' she said scornfully.

'A pity. I'm sure it would have been a delightful experience.' The car drew into the courtyard, making a wide circle round the drive, the evening light casting a rosy glow on the old stones of the house. He glanced at his watch, a little impatiently. 'I'm due out in ten minutes. A drinks party.'

'I wouldn't dream of delaying you a moment longer. I'm sure your name must be top of the social list around here.' Laurie scrambled around for her shopping bags. 'No doubt your County friends are avidly competing for your eminent company, notching up social points for having captured a tame professor.'

'Have you finished? Any other medical problems you want to discuss with me? Any corns, bunions, warts?'

She could not see his eyes. The lights streaming from the Hall were reflected on his gold-rimmed spectacles, turning the lenses to mirrors. He was very still, like a sightless statue.

'I wouldn't bring a baboon to you for help. It would be cruelty to animals. Sorry to have taken up your valuable time, Professor Vaughan. If there is any charge for your professional advice, such as it was, perhaps you'll forward a bill.' She heard him take in a sharp rasp of breath. 'Kindly drop me here.'

He slammed on the brakes and sat still looking ahead, hands gripping the wheel. Laurie opened the door and got out. She was about to turn and thank him icily for the lift, but he leaned over and pulled the car door shut, effectively cutting off her words. He drove off with a great burst of acceleration, spurting gravel.

There wouldn't be any gravel left, thought Laurie, if he went on doing that.

Laurie hurried into Cumthwaite Hall, feeling like an old parcel that had been dumped on the doorstep. She heard low voices and laughter coming from the drawing room, but she did not stop. She did not seek company. She wanted the solitude of her turret flat.

Quietly she put away her purchases. The scatter

cushions were primrose and apricot linen. Laurie stood in
the middle of the room, turning, not quite knowing where
to scatter them. Finally she tossed them on to the head of
her bed. She washed the new mugs and immediately
christened one with a hot coffee.

She tucked herself on to the big floor cushion and
thought about the day—firstly about Milly and then Ben's
obvious contempt and dislike. Nothing ever seemed to go
right between them. He was so rigidly bound up in his
beliefs and medical discipline that he automatically
distrusted anything else. She could understand that but not
why he found it necessary to take out his scepticism on her.

She wished that the rift might be healed. She did not
enjoy being at logged-heads with anyone, but Ben seemed
determined to keep their quarrel fueled—if it could be
called a quarrel. It was more like a battle, she thought, with
sudden amusement as she recalled some of the remarks.
She supposed asking him for a bill was not exactly an olive
branch, but it had been very satisfying. Nor was she going
into the dustbin liner routine again. This time she had been
Milly's advocate and she had nothing to apologise for.

It took her a long time to get to sleep, partly because
Cumthwaite Hall itself did not settle down to sleep until
well after midnight. She could hear voices into the early
hours of the morning—the late-night discussions with
students, putting the world to rights, could go on for hours,
especially if someone brought in a few bottles of wine to
lighten the topic . . .

She tossed and turned as the night dragged on. Her tired
mind began to panic that she would be all washed-out and
unable to work. She knew this wouldn't be true, especially
if she relaxed quietly, but her ragged brain refused to
believe anything that made sense. The duvet had slipped
off and she was unbelievably cold. She knew she ought to
get up and make a hot drink to warm herself, but for some

perverse reason she did not move.

She heard a powerful car coming along the drive and go past Cumthwaite Hall towards the Boathouse. Was it Ben returning late from a tryst, or was it Priscilla arriving early for one? Laurie was too befuddled with tiredness to think straight, she was unhappy that all the lovely promise of working at Cumthwaite Hall could disappear if she was not sensible.

She knew that she must not let this happen. It was in her own hands to stop this heart-searching now. She was here to work, to help people, to promote an understanding of the Alexander Technique. Perhaps tomorrow she would talk to James or Faith and tell them about her difficulties with Ben and her fears for Milly. With that thought and resolution firmly in mind, she fell soundly asleep just before the first bright-eyed herald of the dawn chorus took breath in the tall silver birch trees outside her window.

Laurie coped with a busy day. Her afternoon was fully booked with private students and the amount of energy and concentration she put into it left her white-faced. It was a different sort of tiredness to the heavy backaching, foot pounding slog of ward work. Her mental energy was drained, but she was satisfied that at least she was doing some good.

'Come and have supper with us in the flat,' said Faith as they cleared up the room and put away the treatment tables. 'It's James's turn to cook tonight and he's pretty good. Nothing out of a tin, I promise you.'

'That would be nice,' said Laurie. 'I don't remember when I last ate properly. Except breakfast, of course, which I missed this morning because I overslept. Olive puts out such tempting goodies. But in the evenings, I always seem too tired to do much.'

'About seven then. Don't bother to change.'

But Laurie wanted a shower and it made it more of an

occasion to put on one of her summer dresses. Not that
Laurie had many. It had been pointless to buy a lot of
clothes when she spent most of her time in uniform. But she
had several pretty dresses, expensive ones too, that she had
bought in the sales. All her clothes were expensive and in
good taste. Being on night duty had meant she was often
near the head of the sales queue outside Harrods waiting for
the doors to open. And she always knew exactly what she
wanted and went straight for it.

'I suppose you know what you are looking for in a man
too,' she told herself as the warm water sprayed over her
body. 'Someone expensive and in good taste. But not
someone marked down in a sale. So that's Priscilla's
boyfriend right out. No secondhand goods for me.'

There was a blue flowered silk dress that had always been
a favourite. It had a bloused top and flared skirt; it looked
cool and elegant. Laurie had blue sandals that toned and a
string of opal beads. Her spirits rose as she checked her
appearance in the mirror and decided that she would pass.

'A bit washed out,' she told her reflection, using a dab of
lipstick as rouge on her cheeks. 'But eight out of ten despite
that.'

Laurie found James cooking in the kitchen of the stable
flat, a large butcher's apron tied round his middle. An
aroma of spices and herbs wafted from the pots on the
cooker. Faith was putting out plates and forks and serving
spoons on a low table. It seemed they were going to eat
sitting on the floor.

'Mmn, this all smells delicious,' said Laurie. 'I didn't
realise you were interested in cooking, James.'

'One of my many talents,' he said, lining up raw spring
onions on a chopping board. 'It's how I get rid of my
aggressions.'

'I wonder who's upset him today,' Faith whispered as
James went into the attack with a sharp knife.

'Could it be Professor Vaughan?' Laurie suggested. 'That bully in the Boathouse?'

'Ben been treading on your toes, has he?'

'You can say that again. My feet are pancake flat. It's a wonder I can walk straight.'

'It was the District Council,' said James. 'I got the final rates demand for this place today. I reckon we must be paying for the entire educational programme in Cumbria.'

'Have you heard anything about the lease yet?' Laurie hardly dared to ask but she wanted to know if her unfortunate brush with the owner had ruined all the negotiations. 'Has Professor Vaughan come to any decision?'

James tasted a spoonful of his curry. 'Ben is still sitting on the fence. It's not simply a matter of money, Cumthwaite Hall is the ancestral pile. It's been in the family for ears, and he's very fond of the place though he won't actually admit it. It's hard to imagine him fond of anything—that poker face rarely gives away his feelings.'

'If he's got any,' Laurie murmured.

'And if he sells out to a hotel group, the Boathouse would have to go too,' Faith added. 'They wouldn't want an eccentric professor living on their doorstep, zooming in and out at all hours of the day and night and upsetting their guests.'

'Yes, he'd lose the Boathouse. It would probably be turned into a feature. They would rebuild the old jetty and start a swish sailing club.'

Laurie accepted a glass of chilled grape juice from Faith. 'Thanks. So it doesn't depend entirely on how much he likes or dislikes the school,' she said carefully. 'Or whether I have said the wrong thing to him.'

Faith laughed. 'Don't worry. And don't feel you are to blame. Everyone has upset him at some time or another.

We're always treading on his toes, too. We all do it. It's an occupational hazard around here. Anyway, apparently your apology amused him.'

Laurie had hoped that no one had seen her creeping around in her improvised sackcloth and ashes. 'I'm embarrassed,' she said. 'How did you know? And how much do you know?'

'Ben said something to Olive about a shortage of bin liners up at the Hall. Olive is our two-way grapevine. Nothing is secret. It's a hive of regurgitated gossip. If you want to find out anything, just get Olive talking.'

James started to bring through the steaming dishes—brown rice, saffron rice, a big casserole of prawn curry, side-dishes of sliced bananas, chopped onions, apples, minced hard-boiled eggs, nuts, raisins and coconut. Laurie's appetite returned with a healthy pang of hunger. 'This looks gorgeous!'

'Tuck in,' he said, handing Laurie a plate.

It was a genuine curry, not too hot but a far cry from cold meat heated up in a yellow sauce which St Ranulph's had optimistically served as a curry. Laurie heaped her plate, found a cushion and folded herself round it. It was comfortable and casual. The warmth of the curry and her hosts' friendliness made her feel relaxed and happy.

'You've been looking a bit peaky the last few days,' said Faith. 'We've all noticed. The bloom has gone off our little flower, we said.'

'Little flower?'

Faith laughed again. 'Your face is like a flower, so soft and innocent, petals opening to sunlight and warmth. But you've been drooping lately.'

'Just green fly,' said Laurie. 'I haven't been sleeping well.'

James looked at her intently. 'Have you been overworking? It's easy to do that, especially at first when you are trying to build up private students from scratch, giving them extra time without thinking how much it adds up to in a week.'

Faith interrupted. 'And have you been taking your time off? We don't check you know. We expect our staff to arrange it themselves.'

Laurie tried to remember. 'I'm not sure. Time has gone by so quickly while I've been here. I know I've had two afternoons off because I went shopping in Bowness.'

'You need a proper break,' said Faith. 'A whole day, a whole weekend when you can manage it. Have you been on a lake steamer yet? That would be really refreshing and a wonderful chance to see Windermere's scenery. How about next Sunday then, weather permitting. I'll run you down to Bowness and you can take a full day's tour round Windermere. It's great fun. You could get off at Ambleside for lunch and return later. I'll meet the last steamer back.'

Laurie was amused how Faith was organising everything for her. 'That's very kind of you. It does sound nice. I should get my car back soon and then perhaps I could visit Milly Washbourne. I couldn't stand those two bus trips again. I don't know how she did it twice a day, for a whole week.'

She told them of her fears about Milly, not mentioning that Ben had discouraged her interference. James and Faith were both concerned.

'I could drop by and see her,' said Faith. 'I'll think up a reason. Perhaps she should consult James.'

'And try homeopathic medicine?'

'Don't sound so doubtful,' said James. 'It can be helpful in heart conditions. But we do know our limits. We don't presume to be able to treat a broken leg or a hole in a heart. Our aim is to work alongside orthodox medicine. Even Ben should approve of that. He spends half of his life telling other doctors how dangerous their prescribed drugs can be. No one ever died from taking homeopathic doses.'

'Are there side-effects?'

'Sometimes there is a reaction, but this is part of the healing process, stimulating the body's natural forces of recovery. We are treating like with like, but there is nothing so adverse or life threatening as the side-effects produced by chemical drugs.'

'Oh dear, now you've got James talking homeopathy; he'll never stop. No shop, please, Doctor. Make some coffee for us while I get the Scrabble board out. Would you like a game, Laurie?'

'I'd love one, but I'm a poor player. I've never progressed beyond words like cat and dog. I don't know any of these clever printing terms.'

'It's an art in itself,' said Faith. 'James collects words. He reads dictionaries for fun and I guarantee you'll know some new words before the evening is out!'

Laurie spent a happy evening playing the board game, but she could not help thinking how perfect it would have been as a foursome. She could almost imagine Ben sprawled opposite her, his long legs stretched out, his splendid frame relaxed and comfortable, those beautiful brown hands moving the pieces about, looking up now and then to smile at her.

'Come on, Laurie. Wake up. It's your turn.'

Laurie came out of her daydream with a jolt. Daydreaming now? something she had never done before or had time for. She was changing. Or was it Cumbria that was changing her?

The letters in front of her spelled out the word *love*. She looked at the board but there was no where to put it. It seemed an omen and she felt the unshed tears prickle hopelessly.

'Pass,' she said.

Laurie did not go straight back to her turret flat after leaving the stable block. It was a warm evening and a few minutes stoll would help her to sleep. The garden was alive with the sounds of small rustling creatures, bats swooped through the gloom, somewhere an owl hooted. The wind combed the dark branches and undergrowth, blowing her skirt round her legs.

She recognised the low throb of the powerful engine as it turned into the drive. Ben was returning from yet another party, a part of his life that was a closed book to her. She stepped back into the shrubbery, not wanting to be seen.

The big car came into sight, its metallic body gleaming in the moonlight. Ben was not alone. There were three other people in the car. In the back a young woman and a man, but their faces were indistinct, shadowy. Sitting next to Ben was Priscilla, her hair a silvery cloud on bare shoulders, her head turned towards Ben as her face broke into sudden laughter.

Laurie put her hand to her mouth. Of course Priscilla would have been at the party. She was a local celebrity in her own right. And the perfect partner for Ben—beautiful, intelligent, talented.

She watched the car disappearing towards the Boathouse, then ran to the house and upstairs to her flat. A lot later that night she heard a different car coming from the Boathouse. She knew without a doubt that it was the other couple leaving and that Priscilla was staying alone with Ben.

CHAPTER SIX

FAITH arranged to collect Laurie early on Sunday and Laurie found she was eagerly looking forward to her day out. But when she awoke that morning the crags were covered in mist. It was sheeting down and everywhere was dreary and grey, even the hills seemed weighed down with rain. Slats of rain smeared the windows and obliterated the view.

'Oh no,' she groaned and rolled over in bed, pulling the duvet round her shoulders. It would be pointless to go, even well wrapped up. Instead she would spend the day giving her flat a good clean and using the washing machine in the utility-room next to the main kitchen.

'This fruit needs finishing up, and the milk,' said Olive. She thought Laurie did not eat enough. 'The grapes and melon won't keep. You have them. I'll be bringing in fresh tomorrow morning anyway. Pity to let it go to waste.'

'Thanks,' said Laurie, watching the rain slashing down. 'How kind of you. I'm stuck without my car. I feel absolutely marooned, like being ship-wrecked in mid-ocean.'

Olive did not have quite the same imagination. 'You could go for a walk,' she said. 'You might meet Mr Ben. He's always liked walking in the rain.'

'With Priscilla?' Laurie could not resist saying.

'Aye, maybe, they were always together as youngsters.'

'And now, do they still see a lot of each other?'

'Oh yes. They're very good friends.'

Such a simple phrase but it could mean anything. Laurie did not want to know any more. She had seen them together and that told her everything. They were more than good friends.

The following Sunday was a lovely day, bright and clear with a definite promise of sunshine. Laurie dressed quickly in slim white jeans and a baggy scarlet shirt. She tied her hair back with a striped scarf and ran out to meet Faith in the courtyard.

'It might be a bit crowded,' Faith warned as she drove towards Bowness. 'This kind of weather brings out the day trippers in hordes.'

'I don't mind,' said Laurie. 'It's going to be gorgeous weather. I can feel it in my bones.'

Faith grinned. 'That sounds more like arthritis. I'll give you some Rhus tox. By the way, I might call on Milly this afternoon. I thought I'd leave it a while so it wouldn't look too obvious.'

'How tactful,' said Laurie. 'She's a sensitive person. It must be awful to be old and have people hustling you, and telling you what to do. I don't ever want to be old.'

'There are compensations,' said Faith. 'Especially if you are with the right person.'

Laurie felt a pang of envy. Faith had summed up life itself. If you are with the right person. There was no doubt that this late happiness had settled on Faith like a radiant mantle. The myriad of fine lines round her eyes and her silvery grey hair were not age, just part of a beautiful image.

People were queueing on the jetty to board the steamer; families with excited children in push chairs, couples with their arms around each other, pensioners prepared with thermoses and raincoats. Faith turned away from the sight of so many people.

'I think I'll have a quiet day gardening,' she said. 'Enjoy the Winand.'

'I beg your pardon?'

'He's a Norse hero. Winand or Vinandr. They settled here, you know. Cumbria is a very ancient land, and the lake is called after him. It puts things into perspective for me.'

Laurie did not mind people. Sometimes she liked being lost in a crowd. It gave her a sense of oneness, of disguise, of being unrecognisable. She bought her ticket for a round trip and boarded the steamer. She wandered about, exploring the decks, watching the holidaymakers boarding and bagging seats. Then at last the gate on the lower deck was closed and with a cheerful hoot, the steamer announced its departure. A mild cheer went up as it began to back away from the jetty into the main water, churning a frothy path of wash. The number of craft already on the lake was surprising, flotillas of small boats, cruisers, sailing and rowing boats, speed boats towing skiers.

She wondered if Ben was out in his white cruiser, perhaps taking Priscilla for an early morning trip. They would look well together, one silvery and ethereal, the other so dark and strong. The image was disturbing and she thrust it from her mind.

The shores were well wooded with dramatic mountains in the background and small green islands dotted the water like floating jewels. Fine nineteenth century houses stood in elegant parklands, big handsome Victorian hotels faced the water, strange follies stood on high spots and farmed land in the vales made modest use of the good earth. It was a never-ending scenic panorama. A ten mile water paradise for a maritime population.

The sun came out and Laurie rolled up her sleeves, sunglasses perched on her nose. Everything would be perfect if only she had not met Ben. He nagged at her, like toothache. Thoughts of him would not go away. Suddenly she had a yearning for Ben to be near, to touch her again. If only he were standing here with his arm around her waist, and they were like any other young couple out for the day. It was a pleasant daydream and Laurie was sorry when Waterhead came into sight and they were at the northern end of the lake. She had been warned that Ambleside itself was one mile north of the head of the lake and was jammed with people and traffic. James had told her how to reach the more peaceful parks.

The activity around the jetty was chaotic with craft of every kind manoeuvring the waters; horse-drawn carriages waited to take tourists into town. Laurie wondered how all the boats managed to avoid each other. The steamer had slowed down to almost a standstill, swinging its bulk sideways. Passengers leaned over the rails with eager faces as if they had been away for months on a long sea voyage, not merely travelled from half-way down the lake.

Laurie saw it happen almost before it happened. A young man on water-skis was showing off—he was holding the tow rope with one hand while waving to an admiring girlfriend who was in a rowing-boat in the shallows. It only needed a moment's inattention. The tow-bar slid out of the young man's hand and he lost control, but not speed. Instead of sinking into the shallow water, he careered over the surface straight towards the jetty. It was all over in seconds. He went straight into the concrete pile.

His girlfriend started screaming—a piercing vocal performance. She stood up, rocking the boat alarmingly. Several men ran over and pulled the skier out of the water and laid him on the jetty. Laurie clenched the rail and leaned back. She was not a nurse anymore—she must not rush to help—she must remember not to interfere. She went through the litany twice, trying to convince herself that it was none of her business and there were plenty of better qualified people around to help.

But where were they? Everyone was milling about and the girlfriend was crying hysterically. No one seemed to be doing anything sensible and that had been a terrific crack into the concrete. Laurie could not believe that the skier had got away without injury.

She eased her way along the rail. No, Laurie, she told herself. You are not going anywhere near the accident. You are going to walk right by on the other side. This is your day off. You are going to the park.

Laurie caught her breath sharply. They were doing it all terribly wrong. They were trying to make the poor young man stand up, hauling him to his feet, the blood pouring from his scalp wound. Scalp wounds could bleed in an alarming way because of the abundant blood supply to the head—on the other hand there could be an underlying fracture.

She would telephone for an ambulance. That would be a sensible form of assistance. She pushed through the passengers disembarking and shouldered her way to the jetty. The young man had slithered to his knees and blood was running down his pale chest, mingling with lake water. He looked dreadful. The girl had managed to reach the shore and was running towards him, her hands to her mouth.

None of my business, thought Laurie, hurrying past the gathering, gawping crowd and trying to shut her ears to the girl's shrieks. But it was obvious what the girl was going to do. She was going to fling herself on him and start pulling him about.

'Excuse me, I'm a nurse,' said Laurie firmly and loudly. 'Can you let me through? Please let me through.'

The crowd opened for her and she went down on her knees at the young man's side. She took a quick look at his head. It was a bad scalp wound but he had thick hair and it was difficult to see if any fragments of concrete or wood splinters were embedded. Laurie asked for assistance in laying him down as comfortably as possible. A member of the steamer's crew produced some blankets. The same crewman was sensible enough to go off and phone for an ambulance.

'Ralph! Ralph! Speak to me, darling.' The girl flung her arms round the injured water-skier, and Laurie had a job to prise her off the prone figure.

'Now then, young lady,' said Laurie. 'He's hurt enough without you suffocating him. If you want to be useful, dry his feet and legs. We don't want him losing any more heat.'

The girl looked bewildered, as if the simple task was beyond her. Her face was pale and frightened. Laurie knew that keeping her occupied was the best solution.

'Dry him,' said Laurie. 'With a towel. Ask someone to let you borrow a towel or a handkerchief. Anything will do.'

Someone thrust a bathing towel into her hands and the girl dabbed at his feet, trembling, mouthing his name over and over again. He was not saying much, moaning and groaning, clammy with shock. Laurie examined him gently and was reasonably sure he had not broken any limbs. But the head wound was worrying.

'Are they coming?' she asked the crewman when he returned.

'On their way.'

'Have you a first aid kit on the steamer? I must stop this bleeding.'

'I'll get it.'

It was a standard first aid kit, but it did not have what Laurie needed. A large ring pad. She took a broad sling out of its sterile wrapping and twisted it round and round until it ressembled a doughnut. She positioned the pad carefully over the wound and using another wide bandage began to bind it in place. She had done enough head bandages in training.

'You know what you're doing, don't you?' said the crewman.

'The pressure of the pad helps to stem the blood loss, but doesn't press on the suspected fracture or any bits of concrete. It wouldn't do much good if we just pushed them further in. Haven't you had first aid training?'

'Well, yes . . . but it was some time ago and it's easy to forget. I can just about put on an elastoplast.'

'Very useful in an emergency,' Laurie said dryly. The girl was weeping again, mopping her eyes with the towel, leaving smudges of mascara everywhere. Laurie leaned towards her. 'Keep drying his feet,' she suggested. 'The massage will improve his circulation. You do want to help him, don't you?'

The girl's eyes were awash with tears. 'Is he going to die? He's so p-pale.'

'No, he's not going to die, but seeing you so upset isn't going to help him either. Now pull yourself together, girl. What's your name?'

'Gillian.'

'Okay, Gillian. Now come round this side and dry his hands and arms, and keep talking to Ralph. Tell him he's going to be all right. Be optimistic.'

Gillian sniffed and began patting his arms with the towel, weeping anew at the sight of blood trickling from some cuts and scratches.

'You should be having refresher courses,' Laurie told the crewman. 'You ought to know what to do.'

The crewman grinned. 'We don't get more than the odd nose-bleed or seasickness.'

The ambulance arrived at the steamer pier, siren blaring, lights flashing, and two ambulance men came running with a stretcher. In no time the young water-skier was put on a saline drip, wrapped in warm blankets and transferred to the ambulance.

'Oh no, please don't take him, don't take him . . .' Gillian pleaded, running alongside the stretcher. 'Please, please . . . he's going to die, I know he's going to die.'

'Is she with you?' the driver asked Laurie.

'No, she's not,' said Laurie. 'I don't know either of them. I just happened to see the accident.'

The driver looked at the wailing girl who was clinging frantically to the door of the ambulance.

'She can come along if you come with her, but I daren't risk her having hysterics in the ambulance. She'd be too much of a liability.'

'But I can't come,' said Laurie helplessly. 'I've done my bit. I've helped in the only way I can. Now I want to go.'

'Out of the way please. Let me close the doors now, miss. We want to get going. It's a long way to Carlisle.'

The girl made a sudden dash into the ambulance, flinging herself down on the floor beside the stretcher bed, nearly sending the drip flying. 'Ralph, darling . . . I'll never leave you,' she sobbed.

The driver looked at Laurie and shrugged his shoulders. 'I can't go with an hysterical passenger, you can see that, can't you. And we're wasting valuable time.'

Laurie groaned and picked up her shoulder bag. At least no one had pinched it. 'All right, I'll come. Carlisle? Just my luck. Can't you go anywhere nearer?'

'Shortage of beds, miss.'

She climbed into the vehicle with stiff legs, pulled the girl off the floor and sat her on the opposite bed. 'Calm down, Gillian,' she said. 'Let's have a bit of peace and quiet. You're giving me a headache. So imagine what kind of headache Ralph has got.'

It was a long drive. Laurie had not realised how far Carlisle was. This was the journey Ben did regularly. No wonder they sometimes gave him a driver. She couldn't even see the scenery through the smoked windows. At least there was no chance of bumping into Ben at the hospital, this being a Sunday lunchtime. He would be catching up on his sleep after night duty. She had done enough nights—she knew all about catching up.

She wrapped a blanket round Gillian's shoulders and talked to her quietly about everything under the sun. The tears stopping flowing and there were a few muffled responses.

At last they reached Carlisle, a once prosperous industrial town, with several wool mills. The hospital was solid, red bricked and reassuringly Victorian. There was no wasting time now as the young man was rushed into Casualty and immediately put into a cubicle with nurses and white-coated doctors bustling around.

'Are you a relative?' a nurse asked briskly.

'No, I'm—' Laurie began.

'Then sit over there, please.'

Gillian began crying again, the busy hospital alarming her with its clinical atmosphere of suffering and death. She clung to Laurie, pulling at her sleeve.

'He's going to die,' she sobbed. 'I know he's going to die. Can't you do something?'

'Don't worry. They'll look after him. They know what they're doing. He'll be all right.'

Laurie saw the casualty sister eyeing them again. Had she, too, once spoken to patients and relatives like that? So brusquely and without feeling? She hoped not. Laurie contained a shudder. The white tiled walls were beginning to remind her of another time and it was not pleasant. She felt a familiar wave of panic rising and ran her tongue over a dry mouth.

'Let's sit down,' she said, her voice cracked, her lips unable to close as they trembled. 'We're getting in everyone's way.'

A tall figure stood in front of her, white-coated, stethoscope thrust in pocket. He was so reassuringly familiar that Laurie could have hugged him with relief. But his first words dispelled any warmth of reception.

'Well, look who we have here,' said Ben, glancing down at her with her smouldering eyes. 'If it isn't little Miss Nightingale . . . with a touch of the nervous shakes, if I'm not mistaken. Is the world of real medicine more than you can stomach? Ought I to fetch a kidney bowl?'

Laurie did not answer. It was better to let his snide remarks wash over her.

'Speechless too? This must be one of my lucky days. I am usually subjected to a lecture or a barrage of criticism.'

His voice was mocking as it had been so many times before. It seemed he could not resist seeing how far he could go with his taunts. Laurie let her shoulders relax and her head balance easily, maintaining a poise she was not feeling. She was having enough trouble coping with Gillian, who, on seeing a trolley being wheeled into Ralph's cubicle, had gone completely to pieces. The girl was hunched up on the wooden bench, twisting her sodden handkerchief into shreds, rocking and moaning. But at least the racket took Laurie's mind off her own distress. She massaged the girl's wrist to calm her, to steady the pulse.

'Don't you think this is taking your Girl Guide act a little too far?' he added, swaying back on his heels.

'What are you doing here? I didn't expect to see you,' she countered, ignoring his question. 'I thought you were on nights.'

'I am. This is still night, last night,' he said wearily. 'It's been rather a long one.'

Laurie saw how tired and drawn he looked, his hands

deep in his pockets as if they needed support. A stir of
sympathy came from her own painful memories. She
wanted to take him into her arms and cradle that dark
head, to let him sleep against her breast. She wanted to
watch the lines of fatigue ease from his face. She longed to
feel his breath fanning her skin as he slept. Her wanton
thoughts brought a rush of colour to her cheeks.

'It shouldn't be allowed,' she said in a rush. 'You can't
work when you're exhausted.'

'I really appreciate your concern,' he drawled, standing aside to allow a nurse to go clattering by with another
trolley of instruments. 'But I can hardly tell the patients to
go home. So to what do we owe the pleasure of your
company? Are you with this rather noisy young woman?'

Laura nodded wryly. 'Her boyfriend has been in an
accident. He water-skied right into the pier at Waterhead.
I saw it happen from the steamer.'

'And you just couldn't resist rushing to the scene with a
little eau-de-cologne on your handkerchief.'

Laurie's self control was remarkable. That she had not
done or said anything that would give her previous
profession away, was a consolation. Nor had she betrayed
how happy she had felt, just seeing him.

'I was forced into coming here in the ambulance,' said
Laurie. 'I didn't want to come. I don't know these
people. It's my first whole day off and I'm supposed to be
out enjoying myself, not sitting in this dreary Casualty
Department being put through a third-degree grilling by
a knocked-out, grumpy, bad tempered physician who's
about as sensitive as a . . . as a Brazilian hedgehog!'

Laurie hardly cared what she said. She was so insensed
by his derogatory remarks. His face was hewn out of
granite in the harsh light but then a subtle change came
over him. He seemed to lengthen his back and grow even
taller; he had used the Alexander Technique uncon-

ciously. His eyes softened and he smiled ruefully in a small boy way that was quite captivating. Laurie tried to look away. She was powerless when he turned on the charm. This was the Ben she could easily love.

'Well, we certainly can't have that. Your first whole day off? Something will have to be done to salvage what is left. The young man is in good hands so he's no longer your responsibility. I'll find someone to bring this young lady a cup of tea, and then I think she's big enough to look after herself. I'm going off duty now, so I'll take you home.'

'But I don't want to go home.'

'A Brazilian hedgehog, eh? You must explain the difference of the species.'

'Oh, you're so bossy. It's unbelievable,' said Laurie, despite being relieved that the burden of Gillian was being lifted from her shoulders. 'I don't want to go anywhere with you. I was on a steamer trip, having fun.'

'I'm afraid I can't promise any fun, but how do you think you are going to get back to Ambleside? It's a Sunday remember. Do you want to take a taxi? It would be pricey. You might just as well come with me,' he said with a finality that brooked no further argument.

He strode away, his white coat flapping, scattering nurses and patients as his height and bearing gave him pass power. Laurie was suddenly absurdly proud of him, of his work, his dedication and sheer ability to fit so much into his life. Then she recalled his impossible, dictatorial manner towards her and reminded herself she was no longer a nurse at the consultant's beck and call. She was not there to be told what to do.

'Stay here, Gillian,' she said. 'I'll fetch you a cup of tea. There must be a drinks machine somewhere. Do you take sugar?'

'Thanks,' Gillian sniffed. 'No sugar. And I only drink

coffee.'

'Coffee it shall be,' said Laurie, slightly amazed at her own patience. She went off down a maze of corridors looking for a vending machine.

Laurie and Ben arrived back at the same time, each bearing identical plastic beakers.

'Gillian doesn't like tea,' said Laurie.

'You drink it then,' Ben said curtly, putting the hot beaker down. 'I'll see you round the front of the hospital in five minutes exactly.'

For a few moments she rebelled, then she realised there was sense in taking up his offer. She couldn't afford a taxi and buses, if any, would be a Sunday service. It might take her the rest of the day to get back to Windermere, wandering about all over the countryside. She would be worn out by the time she got back. But she resolved not to get into an argument with him, even if it meant travelling the entire journey in silence.

'Aren't you too tired to drive?' she said before she could stop the words coming out.

He shot her a look of derision. 'I'm not a fool. My driver is booked. He'll drive me home, or wherever we want to go.'

'I don't want to go anywhere,' said Laurie. 'Straight back to Cumthwaite Hall would be preferable.'

'I thought you might like to look at some of our beautiful hills, the ones that Priscilla paints so well. You can't have seen much of Cumbria yet with your car off the road.'

'How do you know so much about me? Who told you about my car?' she retorted, but her head was spinning with anguish. He could not resist mentioning Priscilla's name, it seemed.

'You'd be surprised at the little snippets served with many an early morning cuppa. Olive is a very reliable source. She says there something troubling you. That you don't eat enough. That you seem afraid at times.'

'Heavens, what a lot of fuss about nothing. She's just given me a fright or two. She wears soft soled shoes and I don't always hear her coming. That's all.'

'Just a bit jumpy, eh?' He was regarding her thoughtfully, eyes narrowed. An odd, searching look that made Laurie reluctant to break the spell. 'Perhaps you're working too hard. You ought to go out, get yourself a boyfriend. Most young women of your age, with your reasonable looks, would have acquired a steady boyfriend by now.'

She swallowed dryly, jerking her bag over her shoulder. 'Much as I appreciate your concern, professor, I am not in the market for a medical consultation. Simply a lift, please.'

He shrugged. 'As you wish. Your health is your own business. No doubt the Alexander Technique will come up with something. Or ask Olive to cough loudly. That might have a high success rate in your case.'

Laurie ignored the last remark. She had almost forgotten what it was like to go out with someone. Dates at St Ranulph's with Bruce had been few, from choice on her part. She felt a flicker of pain and it was a warning. She was not ready. She was not going anywhere with Ben. It would only cause trouble. She was going straight home.

Laurie said goodbye to Gillian and the girl did have the manners to thank her. She had calmed down a little and was drinking the coffee. She was going to ring her parents and ask them to fetch her. Even so, she was reluctant to let Laurie go.

The big Mercedes was outside, engine ticking over, the driver at the wheel. Ben was already sitting in the back, hunched, his brief case open on his knee. He was going through some papers, making notes in the margins.

Laurie got in and sat as far away from him as possible, tucking herself into a corner of the roomy seat.

'If you get much further away, you'll be sitting in the boot,' he said without looking up. 'I'm not infectious, you know.'

Laurie did not answer. She had just noticed her jeans, her beautiful white jeans. The knees were spotted with blood and mud and sand. There was dried blood under her nails. She was a mess. She put her hand to her hair, suddenly aware that somewhere along the way she had lost her scarf.

'Would you like to stop somewhere for a late lunch?' he asked politely. 'I don't suppose you've had any, nor have I. I know several nice places on the way.'

'No, thank you,' she said stiffly. She was not fit to eat out, or in company.

'How about some good home cooking? There are several farms round here that do food. It's served in the front sitting room of the farmhouse, quite unpretentious. You don't have to dress up.'

'I'm not hungry. Sorry.'

There was a pause while Ben made a few more notes. They were driving through Carlisle and Laurie glimpsed the famous battered castle, dark and grim, where Mary Queen of Scots had once been kept prisoner.

'The young water-skier is going to be all right. I made some enquiries before we left. All his vital signs were becoming normal. If a fracture shows up on the X-ray, I think it'll be slight.'

'I'm glad,' said Laurie relaxing a little. 'It was certainly a nasty crack he took.'

'The skull is very tough.'

'Those steamer crewmen need refresher courses in first aid,' Laurie went on. 'They hardly knew what to do. Whatever tuition they had was a long time ago and they've forgotten most of it.'

'I'll pass the suggestion on to our Administrator and the St John Ambulance people. Perhaps they'll be able to do something about it.'

He yawned. The warmth in the car was beginning to make him sleepy. It had been a busy night with a rush of intakes from an old peoples' home, all suffering from suspected food poisoning, and a nasty multiple pile up.

Laurie could see him fighting off waves of sleep, so she stopped talking and studied the passing scenery. There were such magnificent views in Cumbria; one never lost sight of dramatic and craggy peaks, rolling hills, sparkling water that glittered and shone with every slanting ray, reflecting all the grandeur around.

Ben had fallen asleep, the pen sliding from his fingers. Carefully she removed the pen and as quietly as possible, put away the papers and closed the lid of his briefcase. He had slipped back against the seat, his face defenceless without its habitual frown, breathing light and regular. She was glad he was not snoring or sleeping with his mouth open. He looked like a dark, brooding giant. She could literally feel the sensation of his body although she was still distanced from him. She moved her cramped limbs and eased a little nearer, wishing she could lean against his arm and close her eyes too.

He gave a slight groan and shifted his long legs, settling into a more comfortable position. He gathered her hand into his grip. How he found her hand without looking, she did not know. She tried to tug away but the hold was firm. He murmured something but she did not catch what he said. His skin was warm and dry and the clasp was reassuring, not threatening in any way. She looked down at his well-scrubbed brown fingers, long and strong, clever and skilled, the hands of a healer.

She dare not move. She did not want the driver to see

them in his mirror, but their clapsed hands were out of his view and Laurie took comfort from that. Ben slept all the way to Cumthwaite Hall; she had not the heart to wake him when she saw the signpost to Ambleside. There was not much of the afternoon left and in her heart she knew she would rather have her hand held in the hand of this sleeping man than be on any steamer going anywhere. It was a strange, magical journey which could have lasted hours or minutes, there was no way of measuring the time. Laurie was grateful and content that for a while, even if he was asleep, they were completely, harmoniously together.

The car turned into the drive of the Hall, and even the familiar sensation of the unmade road did not disturb Ben's sleep. They drew up outside the Boathouse. Laurie had not seen it from this aspect before. It was a timber building, weathered dark brown and old, two-storied, built right over the edge of the lapping water, its ground floor used to store boats, and the upper floor converted into Ben's accommodation.

'It seems a pity to wake him,' Laurie whispered to the driver.

'Flaked out is he?'

'Deader than a dodo.'

'You must explain all these animal comparisons,' came a dry, bemused voice. 'A Brazilan hedgehog and now the dodo. Do you come from a zoological family?'

Laurie tugged her hand away and wrenched at the door handle. But it was an automatic lock and she could not open it.

'That's not fair,' she said. 'Pretending to be asleep and listening to other people's conversations.'

'I've only just woken up,' he said stretching and blinking. He looked as fresh as a daisy. Obviously he had the ability to cap-nap and recoup his energy quickly.

'Thanks, George. You can be off home now. I see you
tomorrow morning. Seven o'clock. I've to be in London
by mid-day.'

'We'll make it, sir.'

'I'll be off too, if someone would kindly unlock this
door,' said Laurie, giving up the struggle. 'Thank you for
the lift home. I am grateful.'

'You can be even more grateful to me and come inside
and fix me a meal while I shower. No breakfast and I
don't remember any supper. I'm so hungry, I'd even eat
your rabbit food.'

George had obviously flicked the right switch because
now the door opened easily. Laurie got out, slim and
defiant, but she hesitated. She did owe Ben something.
He had really been quite kind and she was curious to see
inside his home. It was as if he still held her hand. The
bond, though invisible, was still there.

'All right,' she said. 'But I'm no cordon bleu. It'll be
plain and simple.'

'That's my girl,' he said in a hearty voice that made her
want to hit him.

There was no downstairs. The door opened straight
into a lobby hung with outdoor coats and propped with
boating gear, underwater equipment, wetsuits and water-
skis. She followed Ben up some narrow wooden stairs.
She could see it was going to be a typical bachelor
household—unrestrained chaos.

But she was wrong. She almost gasped with surprise
when she reached the top of the stairs. They walked into a
huge room. It was the whole of the upper floor area of the
building, with wide picture windows and a central
Scandinavian log fireplace made of rough hewn stone.
Everywhere was white and brown. The entire floor was
white carpet, two long sofas adjacent to the fireplace were
upholstered in off-white tweed, a big mahogany desk

faced one window and the wall alongside it was ceiling
high with books. Rich chestnut brown velvet curtains
hung at the windows though Laurie had the feeling they
were rarely drawn.

At the far end of the room was a white ironwork spiral
staircase and a free-standing bookcase with a wall of
hanging plants.

'Take off your jeans,' said Ben, flinging his briefcase
on the desk.

'What?' Laurie was shocked.

'Don't go all maidenly and modest. They are covered
in blood and I'll put them into soak while you have a
bath. Up the spiral stairs and it's the door ahead. You
can't miss it. Help yourself to my bathrobe or find
something that fits. I'll wait until you've finished.'

Laurie went across the soft carpet in a dream. She
wasn't taking off her jeans in front of him. Her brief white
cotton panties were not for his eyes, even if he was a
doctor. She went up the spiral staircase carefully in case it
made her giddy and as she climbed she saw below, behind
the books and hanging plants a very small compact
kitchen area. Above she came straight out on to a
converted loft floor which was just like a ship's cabin. No
king-sized bed for Professor Vaughan. He preferred a
spartan but large and comfortable looking bunk bed with
polished mahogany drawers underneath and a porthole
window at the head. The floor was the same white carpet
and Laurie wondered if the bathroom was going to be
another symphony in white.

It was a surprise, but mainly because of the complete
change of colour. She had been expecting luxury of a sort,
but not the rich dark blue that met her eyes. The big bath,
vanitory unit and toilet were all a deep lobelia-blue. So
were the the tiles and the thick carpet underfoot. The
fitting were brass, but shelving of high-sheen mahogany

held a pile of matching blue towels of all sizes. Her eyes widened as she noticed the controls for a stereo system built into the wall. This was all a far cry from her tiny plastic shower unit.

She turned on the hot water, glad to have the chance to scrub the blood from under her nails and off her body. She slipped out of her jeans and ran to the head of the stairs and dropped them overboard. As they fell, she realised she could have just as easily soaked them in the bathroom but it was too late to retrieve them.

There were no bath salts in the bathroom, nothing feminine at all, which pleased her. Just a sturdy tablet of soap and a nailbrush, although she knew that in the mirrored cabinet were aftershave and deodorant of an expensive brand. She remembered the smell of him in the motorway café.

She took off her clothes and slipped into the hot water. It was bliss. She slid under, letting the water close over her head. It took ages to dry her long light brown hair, but she did not care. She felt hot and gritty and it had to be washed. As she surfaced she heard footsteps coming up the iron stairs. Her glance darted in panic to the towels but they were too far away to reach.

'Don't start screaming,' said Ben. 'My eyes are closed. I've only brought you a drink. Take it before it gets spilled. The thought of a water-nymph in my bath is making me nervous.'

The thought of Ben being nervous was so ridiculous that Laurie laughed. Her fear left her. His eyes were shut fast like a small boy waiting for a treat and he was holding out a glass of wine in a tall, crystal glass. It was so unexpected, she felt her heart leap to him.

'How lovely,' she said, her voice low and husky. 'And how decadent. I don't think I've ever had wine in the bath before.'

'There's only one thing better in the bath,' he said, leaving her to ponder that remark.

She knew what he meant. This bath was big enough for two. She could almost imagine his long legs tangling alongside hers, his toes tickling her thighs. She took a deep gulp of the wine and gripped the nailbrush. These thoughts were ruining her equilibrium. They had to stop! It was almost as if she was having an affair with him, but only in her mind. She lay in a trance of desire, soaping her body, her feelings gathering into such an intensity that it took the utmost concentration to bring herself down to earth and back into Ben's bathroom.

She scrubbed every inch of her skin with operating theatre ferocity. Ralph's blood was gone. The mud and sand from the pier had gone. The sweat and anguish vanished. She came out of the bath as clean as a sprite from a mountain stream. She was small and slim, her skin pearly and glistening. She knew that she deserved some lover to appreciate her yearning body, but there was no one. Bruce was the wrong man and Ben . . . Ben was a million years away.

She slipped on his dark blue bathrobe. It came down to her knees, but she felt enveloped in its hugeness and comfort.

'My turn for the bath,' he said, from the foot of the stairs. 'I hope it's clean.'

'I was trained . . .' she was just going to say something about St Ranulph's but stopped herself in time, '. . . brought up properly.'

By the time Ben came down, scrubbed and wearing clean jeans and a dark sweat-shirt, Laurie had prepared some food. It had not been difficult. His fridge was well-stocked. There were Brussels paté and French Brie cheese; she had made a salad with grated carrot, cabbage, green peppers and celery, wondering who did his shopping. She found brown rolls and warmed them. She took the laden tray through to the coffee table in front of the long sofas, suddenly shy and reserved. They had never eaten together before.

'Dear Laurie,' he said with unexpected understanding. 'Don't look afraid. It's only a meal together. Nothing else, nothing more complicated.' He poured out another glass of wine and offered it to her. 'Here's to some kind of armistice. You and me. Don't you think we deserve it?'

She took the glass from him and was annoyed with herself that her hand was trembling. His fingers curled round the stem of the glass, encasing her own. Keeping the glass steady, he bent forward and quite gently kissed the top of her brow, near her wet hair. 'Oh, Laurie . . .' he murmured. 'Dearest girl . . .'

Laurie felt a flame flickering in her body, this way and that, igniting emotions that had been hidden away so long in her secret mind. She put her hand on his arm, feeling the hard swell of his muscles. The many layers of Ben's character were still unfolding and this dryly humorous, quixotic man, so masculine and strong, could captivate her anytime.

He was going to kiss her. There was no getting out of it. He put down the glass and pulled her slowly into his arms. She felt her heart kicking wildly as his mouth touched her face, her skin, her eyes, moving with sensuous softness towards her lips. Her lips parted, ready for him, feeling his breath warming her. His hands ran over her lightly, tracing her back, curving hips, fingers touching her soft damp flesh. Laurie's craving soared; she lifted herself to his mouth at the same instant that he could wait no longer.

'Laurie,' he breathed. 'Laurie, darling . . . I've been wanting this for such a long time.'

'Oh Ben, this can't be real . . . am I dreaming?' The

words were the merest whisper. She shut her eyes in
ecstasy, it was a whirlwind of sensation that pinioned and
transfixed her close to the heat of his body. She felt the
fastening of the robe loosen as she moved against him, her
almost naked body was fragrant and clean. He lifted her
easily into his arms and carried her to the long sofa, laying
her on the cushions, covering her with his heavy
demanding body.

She opened her eyes lazily, half-dazed, wanting to see
him, stroking his dear dark, crisp hair, tracing the
sideburns tenderly, whispering his name over and over,
as his roaming kisses filled her with delight.

In the gathering gloom she became aware of the
opposite wall. It was a long picture gallery of unsurpassed
beauty. A whole row of framed Cumbrian landscapes
shimmering with a special irridescence that Laurie
recognised instantly. Priscilla's paintings were
everywhere. It was as if the woman was in the room,
filling every corner with her silvery beauty, her ethereal
smile and tinkling laughter. Laurie swore she could smell
the other woman's flowery perfume, hear the swish of her
skirts and light footsteps.

Laurie struggled, pushing Ben from her, trying to sit
up and disentangle their arms.

'I can't, I'm sorry,' she gasped, pulling the robe close
to her breasts, her whole body shaking.

'Laurie, what's the matter? Darling girl . . .' he asked
with concern, at a loss to understand her sudden change
of mood. 'What's the matter? What have I done?'

A shiver passed over her. She took in a great gasp of
breath. 'It's not you at all. It's not your fault. There's
someone else here,' she said. 'I can't compete. I'm sorry,
I really am. It's all a mistake. I must go home. I can't
stay.'

'But there's no one here. We're quite alone.'

'No, no, that's not true. She's here. Priscilla. She's all around. I can sense it. I suppose she was the last occupant of this sofa. Perhaps the other night, when she stayed over.' Her voice rose hysterically. She was seeing that long silvery hair splayed all over the cushions, the mature body rosy in the lamplight.

'What night?' he said coldly. 'I don't what you are talking about. Priscilla is not in the habit of staying overnight. Her morals are impeccable.'

His tone implied that Laurie's were not, or why else was she sprawled half naked on his sofa. It was a terrible insult—shocking and unfair. Laurie staggered to her feet, clutching the robe to her body, her nerveless fingers plucking at a loose thread.

'Don't deny it,' she said hoarsely. 'She didn't leave.'

CHAPTER SEVEN

BEN STARED at her for a long, agonising minute, the flecks in his eyes hardening to granite.

'Don't ever talk about Priscilla like that again,' he said quietly. 'I won't have it. She's a very special person. She's beautiful and talented and I've known her a long time. It's a pity you have such a suspicious mind. I thought for a moment, for a very brief moment, that we were beginning to get to know each other. That it was possible for us to understand each other despite our differences, and not always be fighting.'

'Fighting?' Laurie interrupted. 'Just because—'

'But I was mistaken. We have very little in common. Not even sex. This is not the night for shooting stars.'

'More of a damp squib,' Laurie snapped, unable to resist hitting back. She was furious with him. For making her soft and pliant in his arms, for making her believe him, for tricking her into wanting him. 'What about love? Doesn't that mean anything to you? Or perhaps you don't know anything about love.'

He caught her suddenly against him and tugged at a handful of hair. She felt pain in the roots and went rigid.

'I know about love,' he said fiercely. 'I know how it can eat into your heart, make life either unbearable or a paradise beyond words. But what do you know, little teacher? Has no one taught you how to love?'

He let her go just as abruptly and she fell awkwardly. She had only one thought. To get away.

She was trapped in the middle of a disaster situation. Priscilla's paintings dominated the walls of Ben's living

116

room, making a glowing statement of residential occupation and unspoken ownership of the professor. How had she missed them before? She must have come in, eyes clouded and bemused by the prospect of being alone with Ben. What a fool she was. Maybe they had even made love on this same sofa . . .

It was not a dignified exit. Laurie tried to struggle into her wet jeans in the kitchen—almost an impossibility. Ben tossed out a pair of faded, cut down shorts.

'Put these on,' he said coldly. 'I'll send your jeans over in the morning.'

'No thanks,' she said, avoiding his eyes. 'I'll wear my own.'

'Tell me, are you always so pigheaded? Why don't you trust me? Why are you having hysterics over a few paintings? I collect them. I happen to like them.'

'And the painter!'

'Of course. I rate Priscilla very highly. Something which you don't seem to understand. Or are deliberately trying to misunderstand. I thought . . . oh hell! Nothing you do or say makes any sense.'

'It makes sense from where I'm standing,' said Laurie, trying to balance on one leg to tie up her sneakers. 'I must have been blind. No, I guess I didn't really want to know. I wanted to think you were someone I could trust, someone I could believe in.'

'You're talking in riddles.'

It was a ridiculous conversation. Ben turned his attention to the food and started helping himself as if she was not there.

'Thank you for the lift,' she said.

'You're welcome,' he replied, spreading paté generously on a roll. 'See yourself out, can you?'

'Yes. Of course.'

It was not much fun walking home across the parkland in

wet jeans. Laurie stumbled, nearly falling over a stray ram
that had wandered into the grounds. She scolded herself for
reacting so violently to the paintings. She just could not
help it; Priscilla was everywhere. Laurie hoped she would
never see Ben Vaughan again. That seemed the answer to
everything.

She began her private work the next afternoon after a
busy morning with a new set of students. She saw from the
appointments book that she had been given a young girl to
see, Trudy. When the girl walked in, Laurie was
immediately interested for two reasons. It was obvious she
had lordosis, a postural deformity of the spine, and a neck
twist. And secondly, Laurie was sure that she had seen her
somewhere before.

The girl had brought a letter. It was typed on Carlisle
County Hospital headed notepaper, signed by Professor
Ben Vaughan with a bold black pen. He was asking Laurie
to treat Trudy's spinal condition and to send the account to
him personally. It was dated the previous Friday.

Laurie was completely thrown. She had to go over to a
window and stare at the windblown trees by the lakeside.
Ben was actually asking her to treat one of his patients.
She could hardly believe it. He could not feel the
Alexander Technique was a complete waste of time if he
was sending her a student, and an impressionable young
girl at that.

She turned to the girl, her eyes warm and welcoming.
'Well, hello, Trudy,' she said. 'Come and tell me about
yourself. Tell me about school first, and your hobbies and
the sports you do.'

The girl was reluctant to talk. It seemed she was at
Cumthwaite Hall under protest. Laurie explained in
some detail to the girl how she could help correct the
misuse of her spine, how the way she carried her satchel
was not helping her neck.

'I don't know. It all sounds funny to me. My friends will laugh at me if they find out I'm coming here,' said Trudy reluctantly. 'But I do want to be a model. And I'm mad about clothes. I like the way models walk about to disco music, wearing smashing clothes. I'd like to do that.'

'There's no reason why you shouldn't become a model. You have a lovely face, but you've a forward curvature of the spine which won't exactly help your career.'

'And can this Alexander Technique thing help my spine? Is it going to hurt? I didn't like physiotherapy much.'

'No, it won't hurt and yes, it can help. Why not give it a try? And you are young enough to learn very quickly. You haven't had time to acquire all our bad habits.'

The girl grinned impishly and tossed back her ponytail. It was then that Laurie remembered where she had seen Trudy before. She was the schoolgirl who had helped retrieve the contents of Milly's handbag from the pavement. Laurie did not mention it, but she was glad she had placed the girl.

'Have you any idea why Professor Vaughan has sent you to me? Laurie asked carefully. 'Did he say?'

'Nope. He said it was some new-fangled idea. He said it wouldn't hurt to give it a try.'

'Hardly new-fangled. The technique has been around nearly a hundred years. It's just so revolutionary that it takes time to learn and to spread.'

'Did you have to learn it?'

'Of course. First I was student myself, wanting primarily to strengthen a painful back, then I became so interested that I enrolled in a three year course to be a teacher. Fortunately I had the kind of job, working shifts, that meant I could do both at once.'

'In a factory?'

'Sort of,' Laurie smiled. She was not having this young lady going back to Ben with any clues about her nursing career. It would only add fuel to the fire of his scorn. 'I know its difficult to understand how the technique works at first so let's have a little demonstration of how thought works.'

Laurie stood about a yard in front of Trudy and smiled encouragingly. 'I am thinking in my head about standing.'

Trudy's young face was a picture. She obviously thought Laurie was a complete freak.

'I want you to push me. Go on, push me over.'

Trudy was convinced that Laurie was a nut case now, but if she wanted to play games . . . she gave Laurie a push that sent her staggering back a few paces.

'Okay,' said Laurie coming back to her original position. 'Now I'm thinking about standing again, but this time the thought is lodged in my pelvis. Push again, will you?'

Trudy grinned. She gave Laurie a push mid-shoulder, but Laurie hardly moved. She pushed again. Laurie was as firm as a rock, her eyes twinkling at Trudy's amazement.

'You see we have a stronger balance when the weight is lower down. No tricks, no strings, I promise. I did nothing but think it. Let's try the same thing out on you.'

They reversed roles and the thought process worked on Trudy as well. She showed the first signs of real interest.

'I'm going to try this on all my friends. It's fun,' she said. 'Show me some more.'

'That's the trouble,' said Laurie ruefully. 'It's hard to show people when it's a technique of non-doing. It's like snow slipping off a leaf . . . you have to have a feeling of detachment. The teacher guides your muscles into the right position and tension, then the experience becomes familiar.'

'I don't think I'm going to be any good at this . . .'

'I'm going to show you the semi-supine position first which you should do for seventeen minutes every day.'

'Oh yoga and meditation, you mean.'

'No, it's neither. It's a way of putting the fluid back into your discs. You don't have to meditate. You can listen to music, listen to the birds . . . anything. Climb up on to the treatment table and let me show you how to place your feet and hands. Don't look so worried. It won't hurt!'

Trudy was a pliant pupil, easy to guide and direct. Laurie knew that they could work together and make progress.

So Ben had sent her a challenge in the shape of Trudy. By the end of their first session, Laurie felt that she had gained Trudy's tentative interest, and she booked an appointment for her at the end of the week for another lesson.

As was usual at the end of the day, Laurie went to the kitchen to make a cup of tea, looking forward to a few moments for relaxation. She was not pleased to see Ben hurrying across the courtyard, his face pre-occupied. He was the last person she wanted to see. He was in his trucker's gear, black leather jacket and black jeans, heavy boots. He looked as if he had urgent business to attend to, no time for pleasantries. Light was fading and a keen wind was rising from the ruffled water. Laurie shivered.

'Where's Olive?' he asked abruptly.

'She's gone, long ago.'

'Hell!' He turned on his heel, and then immediately swung back. 'Can you get a thermos of hot coffee, soup, anything. And quickly. There are some young lads stranded on Great Gable. They may be injured. They are certainly suffering from exposure.'

'Yes. We've thermoses galore. Anything else, sir?

Sandwiches, fruit, chocolate?'

'I don't want a menu, Laurie, just get moving. There's no time to waste. We want to find them before the light goes.'

He was bossing her about again, but Laurie obeyed instinctively. This was an emergency. She ran into the kitchen and put on the electric kettle. She got a basket and filled it with fruit, rolls and cheese. Her walking boots were in the lobby, waiting to be cleaned. She pulled them on and grabbed her anorak. By that time the water was boiling, and she made up a thermos of coffee and another of tomato soup. Basket full, she ran out to Ben's car. He was in the driving seat, the engine running.

She got in beside him. 'I've got everything.'

'Thanks. But you're not coming.'

'I am. I could be helpful.'

'Please get out.'

'Another pair of hands,' she said primly.

'You'll only be in the way. A liability.'

'You think you're the only one who can do anything around here,' she insisted. 'I assure you that I won't get in the way and won't attempt any climb beyond my ability. I'm simply coming along as back-up.'

He groaned with exasperation. 'Làurie, you're a menace. What am I going to do about you? I haven't the time, damnit, to argue.'

'Then take me along.'

He put the car into gear and accelerated. His profile was stern and unrelenting. She had offended him again. Still, she was getting used to that.

'Lights,' said Laurie, reminding him.

He said something vicious under his breath which Laurie did not catch and switched on the side-lights. It seemed he was not going to mention her sudden embarrassing departure from the Boathouse, but Laurie had to say something.

'About last night,' she began, searching for words.

'No post mortems,' he said. 'It didn't happen.'

'But I want to explain.'

'I'm not interested in any explanation you might have to offer,' he said, not taking his eyes from the road. 'I obviously made a mistake, for which I apologise. The incident is closed.'

He drove through Windermere and down into Bowness. They did not have long to wait for the ferry across to the other side of the lake, then they took the road to Seathwaite.

'Where are the boys?' she asked, breaking a long silence.

'Near Kern Knotts Crack on Great Gable. It's one of the classic climbs and a constant challenge to all and sundry. People are always getting stuck half-way up or half-way down.'

'You're not going alone, are you?'

'Of course, not. Show some sense. The team is already on its way. There's word that one of them is injured so I'm needed on the spot. It's a steep climb but there are wonderful views.'

'Not this evening,' said Laurie, suppressing another shiver. 'The mist is coming down. I don't like it.'

'There's still time for you to go back. I'll drop you off at Seathwaite.'

Laurie heard the finality in his voice and her heart fell. He did not want her. He never had. It was all in her overactive imagination and the fraility of her body. All she could understand was her own lurking hunger for this man, and how deeply he kindled her desire. She had been betrayed. Betrayed by the fire of her own body. The warmth of his kisses had been her downfall.

'No, thank you,' she said, gripping the handle of the

basket. 'I don't want to be dropped off. I'm coming with you.'

'I do know how to pour soup. I can cope.'

'More surprises! Not just the handsome doctor. Not just a smooth bedside manner,' Laurie said. 'Handy with a thermos, too. Wow! Where do your talents end?'

'I've been a bachelor for long enough to drown in soup.'

A pang shot through her as she heard him chuckle. His mood had changed again. One minute he was aggressively cutting and hurtful, the next friendly and full of boyish charm. No wonder she was confused.

'Thank you for sending Trudy along to see me,' she said, not knowing what she wanted anymore. 'I'm sure I'll be able to help her once I've gained her confidence. She's a nice kid. Does this mean you've seen the light at last?'

'Never. I thought it would be interesting to see what you could or could not do. It's not really a job for orthodox medicine.'

'No, you can't really straighten out arched spines, can you?' she said sweetly. 'Or prevent them. You'll see a change in Trudy, I promise you that. Wanting to be a model is a good incentive, as long as she doesn't start sticking her hips forward and waggling them as she walks. That would be just as wrong.'

'Your problem, not mine,' he said. 'Just send me the bill.'

'With pleasure.'

'Here we are, Seathwaite. Thwaite is Norse for a clearing in the forest,' he added. 'Did you know that?'

'Not another lecture,' she said. 'I'm not studying for an O-Level in Norse.'

He parked the big car, folded away his specs and took out a walkie-talkie set. In moments he was in contact with the rescue team. The static crackled and then a man's voice came over giving Ben information as to where the climbers were and their condition.

'Okay, let's get going,' he said, heaving his medical bag over his shoulder. He caught sight of Laurie's laden basket. 'What have we got here? Little Red Riding Hood?'

She looked at him with suspicion, tempted to make a wisecrack about looking for the lonesome wolf and she would have done if she had been with Bruce or any of her friends at St Ranulph's. But her humour quailed in Ben's company. She could not make a sexy joke, however innocent.

She followed him out of the car park, eyes on the ground, determined not to utter a single grumble as they climbed towards the Great Gable. Her walks in the Lake District had been the easier ones. She had never attempted anything remotely difficult.

'This is Sour Milk Ghyll,' he said, striding ahead.

'All these funny names,' she panted.

'Dollywagon Pike, Combe Gill, Swallow Scarth, Lanty Tarn, Striding Edge, Crinkle Crags.' He rattled them off like a litany, but Laurie could hear the affection in his voice. 'They are a kind of poetry in themselves. Can you hear it?'

'You love it here, don't you?'

'Yes, I wouldn't want to live anywhere else. It means I have to do a lot of travelling, but coming home to the Lake District is worth it. Where is your home?'

'Home?' Laurie was taken aback as he swung round, his large stature blocking her away. 'I don't really have a home. I'm sort of a respectable vagabond. I've never had anywhere before to call my own. I can get everything I own into my car.'

'Don't shack up with the wolf then,' he said, tapping

her basket. 'That would be a mistake. Wait for his big brother, far more trustworthy.'

'One wolf is as bad as another.'

'And the wolf shall also dwell with the lamb,' he quoted.

'I don't believe . . . a word of it,' she wheezed, falling behind.

'Are we stopping for a breather? Lost your puff?'

The landscape was already becoming awesome. The rugged profile of volcanic rocks was spectacular, the far off crags like a smouldering grey dream. Darkness was settling on the fells and the ankle-deep bracken was turning purple. But as they climbed the track became more barren and wild, eroded by the wind and rain, crags and gullies bereft of any growth.

'Do you know where we're going?' Laurie asked, her feet slipping on the shale.

'Hey, you've had enough,' he said, steadying her arm. He noted the dew of perspiration dampening her fringe. 'Slow down. There's a big rock over where you can shelter. Make a fire on a ring of stones. I'll leave you some matches. You'll be quite safe.'

'You're not leaving me are you?' said Laurie, trying to keep the anxiety out of her voice. 'I couldn't stay here on my own.'

'I didn't make you come along,' he pointed out. 'It's steep from now on. We don't want two accidents. You'd be better off waiting for us to return. I'll take the coffee and the soup.'

Her hair was blowing across her face. They were so high up, she felt they were almost flying. She did not want to be left behind, the height scared her, but as usual, Ben made sense. She would only be hindrance. She would have to wait by the rock.

'Where's your famous Girl Guide spirit?' he said more

gently. 'Practise fire lighting.'

He bent and tipped her chin. Their lips were touching, their thighs close. Before she could collect her wits, he was pushing tendrils of hair from her face and touching her skin with small delicate kisses. The sensation made her melt, make her toes curl, made her lose her senses in a terrible need for him.

'I'll be back,' he said, giving her a little push towards the rock. 'Don't run away.'

She did as she was told, hiding her fear and her tears. She was going to be terrified, out here alone in the open, half way up a mountain in the growing darkness. But it was her own fault. She had insisted on coming along. She could just as easily have stayed at Cumthwaite Hall or sat in his car at the car-park.

Ben settled his bag more comfortably on his back and with a nod, took off along the narrowing track. It was ascending more steeply, following the base of a crag and disappearing into the mist. At some point he switched on a powerful torch and she watched the speck of light till that too vanished.

Someone had made a fire before near the rock and there was already a ring of stones and some grey ashes. She hunted around for twigs and dry bracken, and soon a small fire caught and the flickering flames cheered her spirit. As her eyes became accustomed to the dark, she realised she was not the only one on the mountain; there were other wavering lights and she thought she caught snatches of men's voices on the wind. It could only be the rescue team, and her fear was forgotten as she thought of their courage as they scaled Kern Knotts Crack in the darkness.

She hugged her anorak around her and fed the little fire, thinking of Ben. He was an amazing man. Did he ever stop working, helping people? He would do nothing by halves, whether it was loving or hating a person. But how could she tell if he cared for her? Those kisses had merely been a way of quelling her nerves, a reassurance, she knew that. Ben being a doctor, not a man.

She did not know how long she sat there, drinking in the beauty of the darkening mountains, not afraid anymore, completely certain that Ben would be back for her. She had only to wait.

Dots of light appeared first, then came voices. The team was straggling down the mountainside. She stood up with an overwhelming desire to run and meet them. But she did not move, her heart seeming to swell with sudden anguish, her pulse racing. Supposing he was not there? Supposing he had been hurt, fallen down the steep face of Kern Knotts Crack and was even now badly injured?

'Ben,' she whispered. 'Ben . . .'

He came out of the gloom, straight towards her. He put an arm around her slim waist, pulling her to him. She buried her face in his shoulder. He smelt of sweat and mud, but it was all man. All Ben. And he was safe.

'Oh Ben, I thought you might be hurt. I thought you might have fallen. It's so dark, so steep and slippery . . .'

'All this thinking,' he teased. 'It's not good for you. I know these mountains too well to fall.'

There were two youths among the men. They were walking slowly with assistance, one limping, the other was heavily bandaged under his coat. The arm of his injured side was being supported in a sling.

'They are both doing pretty well,' said Ben, following her gaze. 'They tumbled down together. One fell on the point of his shoulder, but he kept his nerve, despite the pain, while the third lad went for help. They were glad of the coffee and soup.'

'Fractured clavicle is it?' Laurie asked, noting the way the boy was inclining his head.

He nodded. 'We'll get them both to hospital for X-rays as soon as possible.'

'Is it just one collar-bone broken?'

'He's walking. He'd be on a stretcher if both had gone.'

'It must be difficult to transport a sitting case down a mountain.'

'We've done it before.' Ben's voice had become stony.

His arm dropped from her waist and he went back to his patients. Laurie felt a chill where his arm had been and wondered what she had done that he had suddenly detached himself from her.

The rescue team gathered round, converging on the basket of food like homing pigeons, tired faces glistening in the firelight. The climb had given the men appetites as most of them had missed suppers. They demolished the refreshments in minutes, cheerful and animated that their mission had been successful.

'Thanks, miss,' they said. 'That was great.'

'You're welcome,' she murmured.

Ben took nothing. He did not come near her again but stayed a distance from her. She tried to keep up an easy conversation with the other men, but all the time her heart was aching for Ben to come back to her. The stars were beginning to puncture the velvety sky with their brightness but she could not admire their beauty when she felt so desolate.

They continued the trek down, the two injured climbers valiantly making as little fuss as possible. Laurie slowed her pace to keep them company, making sure the bandages had not loosened and that the boy's helpless arm was properly supported.

They were both hungry but Ben warned them not to eat before they reached the hospital. It was a wise precaution in case either of them needed an anaesthetic.

At last they reached level ground where the ambulance men were waiting. Ben saw the two boys into their care and

then, after a few words with the team leader, he walked
towards the car-park.

'You're not going with them?'

'No, my job's finished. I'm not on duty tonight.'

The darkness seemed to be splintering around her.
Laurie did not understand what was happening. She
seemed unable to speak or move normally. She tried to
think of her technique but everything had left her. She
was strung up and tense, like a doll on wires.

'Are you coming?' he said, his eyes boring into hers.
'I'll take you home.'

'Yes . . . thank you,' she said huskily. She seemed to be
lost in a silence of anxiety.

'Give me the basket.'

Laurie hung on to the handle. He was talking to her as
if she were just an acquaintance, someone he had met in
passing. What had happened to those kisses, those tiny
kisses raining on her face? Had she dreamed it? The tall,
dark man had no gentleness for her now. He was back to
his trucker arrogance. It was like a douche of cold water, a
devastating feeling.

'What's the matter?' she asked, not able to keep quiet a
moment longer. 'What have I done wrong now?'

His fist hit the roof of his car, and he turned with a face
so forbidding that Laurie shrank from him.

'A fractured clavicle. A sitting case. A ring pad on the
injured water-skier. That concern for your elderly friend.
The professional touch. I should have known,' he said
curtly. 'You're a nurse. A trained nurse. You're one of
the reasons why wards close and patients get turned away.
What the hell do you think you're doing at Cumthwaite
Hall, wearing a pretty track suit and playing at healer.
Your place is in a hosptial, doing what you were trained
for, not dabbling with fringe beliefs.'

'Oh, that's nice,' said Laurie trembling, fury blazing

in her eyes. 'Blame me for the entire NHS fiasco. All right, so I am a trained nurse, and good one, but what do you know about the work? What do you know about the long gruelling hours, the menial tasks, the pittance for pay? Nothing, absolutely nothing. You're a high and mighty doctor, used to having whole regiments of nurses at your beck and call, night and day. Yes, doctor, no doctor. Certainly doctor. Oh yes, you work hard and I don't doubt you were poorly paid at first. But you've left all those days behind now. Conveniently forgotten in all the glory. You don't see nurses driving around in Mercedes and buying valuable paintings for a hobby. You try living on what I earned.'

'The money, always money. I should have guessed it was financial greed,' he scorned. 'I thought nursing was supposed to be a vocation. No one goes into it for the money. What about your training and how much it cost society to put that knowledge into your head? It costs thousands to train a nurse; your experience is invaluable to society. And you're throwing that all away, carelessly and without conscience. Just for money. You ought be be ashamed of yourself.'

He went round to the other side of the car, shoulders hunched, the planes of his face in shadow. His voice was harsher than she had ever heard before, painfully grating, but she could not let the unfair accusation pass.

'So you think it's all about money! That's a laugh!' Laurie nearly spat the word at him. 'That's all you know. I'm not exactly earning a fortune teaching the Alexander Technique. It isn't in the business of making money. But I am regaining a pride in my work, and I do feel I'm doing something worthwhile. I wasn't trained just to be a waitress, to be a bed-maker, to trundle bedpans backwards and forwards to the sluice. Fighting for more beds, for decent staff, even for basic supplies. That's not nursing or patient care. Nor is filling in piles of forms half the night.'

'Oh, you can write, can you? What an asset you must have been.'

She bristled with disgust. 'You are so rude, so insolent, Professor Vaughan. It's unbelievable. I'm not surprised you're still a bachelor. Who would want to live with you? Who could stand your arrogance and stupidity, yes stupidity, for five minutes, let alone a lifetime? No wonder Priscilla puts half a lake between you. She has more sense.'

His rugged face was rigid with anger. Laurie knew that nothing would ever be right again. She had blown it. She leaned against the car door, the world spinning around her, all emotion draining from her veins. Her failure weighed like an iron yoke, constricting her throat. She knew from those moments on the mountain that she loved him but it was too late. Her new knowledge slipped into deep grief. She loved him and had thrown everything away in a pointless argument. Why hadn't she told him about her nursing earlier, in a more rational moment, not at the end of a long day when they were both exhausted.

'My personal life is my own business. I don't need this aggravation,' he said with a coldness that frightened her. He looked shattered, his skin grey. 'I've a full day tomorrow and I'm going home for a good night's sleep. But I'll think of you the next time we have to turn a patient away because of a shortage of staff. Kindly get in the car and keep quiet.'

'I'll get a taxi.'

'Oh, not that all over again,' he thundered. 'You are the most infuriating woman I have ever met. Won't you ever learn? If you don't do as you are told, I might just drive off and leave you stranded.'

Laurie hesitated. She wanted desperately to fling away

from him and find her own way home. But it was a foolishness. She was frightened and it was dark. She did not know where she was, let alone if there was any public transport.

She wrestled with the door handle and got into the passenger seat, hugging the basket on her knees, feeling faintly sick. He started the engine and backed the car out of the car-park. He drove in silence, slower and more deliberately than usual, as if he was aware of his own fatigue. She could appreciate his point of view, that of a man high in the medical profession, but he was not even trying to see hers. He could only see the waste of training. But he did not know how she had struggled on those last three years, trapped by her own fear and guilt. How her life had disintegrated in a nightmare she could not forget.

She got out on the ferry ride across the lake, letting the wind blow away the cobwebs as she leaned on the rail. The water smelt fresh and tangy. Low lights on the woodland shores twinkled like fairy lights, so pretty and remote, so different from the torches on the mountain. They did not represent people or homes, just fairies.

It was a relief when the car turned into the drive, now a familiar and a homely sight. Ben drew up outside the Hall and pulled on the brake. He turned to her, his hair dishevelled, his faced streaked and muddy, dark with stubble, eyes glazed with fatigue.

He already regretted what he had said to Laurie in the heat of the moment. He did not understand what had got into him. He knew she was a kind and caring person with a vein of steel in that fragile-looking body. He knew she had not left nursing for the money. She hardly had any. She drove a clapped out old car. Her clothes were good but she had very few. He had watched her many times walking alone in the grounds, staring out across the lake, keeping well away from his wall. Often he had wanted to join her, but she seemed to have an air of isolation that deterred him. And his own status and success were a barrier in themselves.

'Would you like to come to Amsterdam with me,' he said suddenly. 'I'm speaking at a European Conference next weekend. They've invited me and my wife. And since, as you have so succinctly pointed out, I don't have one, you might as well come. It seems a pity to waste the air ticket.'

She caught her breath, shaking her head in disbelief. 'If that is supposed to be a joke, I'm afraid I don't see anything remotely funny in it,' said Laurie.

'I thought you might learn something from being in a different environment for a few hours. You might stop thinking about yourself and your pride, and remember the rest of humanity. Particularly those that are suffering.'

'What a lot of pompous twaddle. You must be joking.'

'I'm perfectly serious. It could help to get things in perspective. You seem to have such a low opinion of the medical profession and my work. Adverse drug research is vital.'

'I never—' she began.

'Please don't interrupt. I feel you should sit in on one of my lectures and be reminded of what real medicine is about. Not standing properly is hardly life threatening.'

Laurie swallowed a ready retort. How could he be so pompous and condescending . . . she frowned, trying to remember her student days. She had worked and studied so hard that most of it was now a kind of blur. 'I think I've already been to one of your lectures, when I was training at St Ranulph's.'

'Yes, I have lectured at St Ranulph's. And you don't remember a word of it?'

'I was always tired,' she said, excusing herself. 'I

probably dozed off.'

'Obviously one of my better efforts,' he said, with a glimmer of amusement. 'Soporific. All the more reason to come to Amsterdam and stay awake through one.'

'I'm sorry but it's out of the question. There's absolutely no way you and I could get along for a whole weekend even if I wanted to go. And as for going as your wife, that really is an insult. You have such an inflated opinion of yourself. I wouldn't be seen dead as your wife.'

'There you go again, jumping to conclusions,' said Ben, exasperated. 'I didn't say anything about taking you along as my wife. I merely said that they had sent two air tickets, one for my wife. They have also booked me a room at the Hotel Alkmaar but I can phone and book a separate room. Amsterdam is a picturesque city and you would enjoy a cruise along the canals or a visit to the floating flower market. I shall be busy at the Conference. We need not spend any time together.'

Laurie wondered why on earth he was asking her to go with him. He had been so angry with her. Did he really think that attending a medical conference would convert her back to bedpans and night duty? She had half a mind to go and then tell him afterwards that all the stuffy ideas and opinionated people she'd met had more than confirmed her decision to leave nursing.

'Could I be sure of that?' she asked. 'Could I have it in writing?'

'What a firecracker, you are,' said Ben, half-laughing. 'You look so quiet and demure, that pale brown hair, pale hazel eyes, luminous skin . . .' he brushed the back of a finger against her cheek, electrifying her. 'But inside you are a volcano, erupting without warning, shooting sparks of fire at the slightest provocation. You ought to wear a DANGER badge—"Liable to explode at any moment". Laurie, you would have made a damned fine matron, everyone trembling at your feet.' Suddenly he grabbed a handful of her hair. 'Are you sure this isn't really red? Have you dyed it?'

'Don't be ridiculous,' she said, pulling her hair out of his grasp. 'You can't dye red to washed out-brown.'

'It's the colour of some little bird,' he mused. 'A sparrow or a wren or something. I don't really know birds. You're the expert on animals. Brown as a dodo?'

'Dodos had short stout legs and greyish plumage. Flightless and now, alas, defunct. It also refers to an intensely conservative person who is unaware of changing ideas.'

She could not resist that last dig, even though she ached to go with him. She stared into the darkness, trying to decide what to do. If only she could restore some good feeling between them, though she was not stupid enough to think that there could ever be anything as strong as love. Commonsense told her to refuse, forget the Professor, get on with living her own life, keep her feet firmly on the ground.

'A separate room?' she said, off-hand.

'A separate room.' He stiffled a patient sigh. He longed for his bed. He did not understand himself, trying to talk this obstinate girl into going to Amsterdam. He was not even sure now that he wanted her to come.

'All right,' she said, sounding clumsy and ungracious. 'I'll come.'

CHAPTER EIGHT

AMSTERDAM was a fascinating city even in the darkness. Laurie sat on the edge of her seat in the taxi, absorbing all the new sights and sounds and scents, her face aglow with interest. Ben could not keep his eyes off her. She was like a small girl on an outing, her soft grey eyes so clear and lambent, quite different from when she was angry and they sparked fire.

She caught glimpses of canals, stone bridges and the tall old gabled houses, windowboxes spilling with flowers. She turned to Ben, conscious of a tremendous excitement. He was so big and rugged in a mole-coloured suede jacket, crew-necked jersey, well-cut trousers—he made her feel safe. She knew that nothing could happen to her while he was by her side. If only Ben had been around that evening, that other evening . . .

Laurie had deliberately dressed down for the flight, not wanting Ben to think that the weekend was important to her, or that he was important. She was in her oldest faded jeans tucked into boots, with a baggy T-shirt and blouson jacket, her hair in a thick, glossy plait.

The taxi stopped outside a large solid Edwardian hotel with a gabled slate roof and grey stone walls. It looked homely and respectable, a little plush but very comfortable.

'How very respectable,' Laurie murmured as she pulled out her weekend bag. 'Don't tell them that I'm not your wife. We might get thrown out.'

'In Amsterdam?' He raised his dark eyebrows, reminding Laurie that Amsterdam's code of morals was liberal by any standard and its nightlife sophisticated. She coloured faintly and looked away, pretending to admire a colourful display of flowers in the foyer, begonias and carnations in riot.

'Don't worry. 'We're booked in our own names, and if anyone asks who you are at the conference, I shall simply tell them the truth.'

'Will you tell them I'm a friend or an adversary?' said Laurie mischievously. 'Bombarding the barricades.'

He lowered his head towards her, till his warm breath scanned her skin. 'Neither. I shall say you are a colleague and a neighbour. Will that suit you?'

'How boring. No one will be surprised if we ignore each other throughout the entire proceedings.'

'We probably will. I shall be busy as I like to attend the other lectures and I've people to see. One never stops learning at any age.' There was an inflexion of sarcasm in his voice which Laurie did not miss. 'You might like to go on a canal cruise in the morning, then my lecture is at two o'clock in the afternoon. Don't miss it.'

They entered the brass and mahogany panelled lift, Ben juggling the room keys in his hand as if he was undecided which one to give her. He got out at the second floor and handed her a key with a silent nod.

'It's late and I've some notes to look at. Your room is on the top floor. Perhaps I'll see you at breakfast. Goodnight, Laurie.'

'I suppose you are one of those calm and collected clever clogs who can eat a hearty breakfast and a three-course lunch before giving a lecture to a hundred people.'

'Nearer five hundred. All the EEC countries are represented. No, I get apprehensive, just like any human being. Don't credit me with nerves of steel. Things can go wrong. I could go a total blank, drop my notes, trip over the steps. Once I forgot where I was and welcomed the wrong hospital staff.'

'Easily done,' said Laurie with a gentle smile. 'Especially if you've been travelling around.' She wondered how much she could say, if she dare mention ways that would help him. She did not want to spoil the evening's pleasant atmosphere. 'Can I talk shop?' she added, finding some courage.

'Oh dear,' he said, but he looked more amused than annoyed. 'Not another artillery barrage?'

'Just a short burst. I know how I feel when I have to take a class on my own. Just as I am about to start, my neck gets tense, hands perspire, heart beats go faster, helter-skelter thoughts. Then I discovered that these stress reactions actually start a lot earlier and are a chain that can be prevented. I was able to decide not to tense my neck, not to contract my calf muscles, to keep my thoughts clear, still and in order.'

'What a sweet little teacher you are,' he said giving her plait a playful tug. 'I wish I'd had a teacher like you.'

'In other words, concentrate on the present experience and stop worrying about the future,' she put in quickly.

'Point taken. I think I'll concentrate on going to bed. Goodnight, Laurie.'

'Goodnight, Ben. And . . . and thank you.'

'Don't mention it. My pleasure.'

He walked away, slightly stooping, and Laurie knew without a doubt that she had fallen blindly, irrevocably in love with the man. Every inch of him was so precious that she longed to draw him into her arms, to comfort him, to be tender and loving. She ached to touch the dark hair curling at the nape of his neck, to run her hands over those strong, broad shoulders . . .

Abruptly she pressed the button for the top floor and the lift door closed, cutting his tall figure from view. As she suspected, Ben had given her the double room. It was high up overlooking the city, the broad windows giving a superb

view of twinkling lights and glistening water. She
explored the comfortable room, testing the bouncy bed,
feeling the thickness of the towels in the bathroom,
flicking the televsion on and off. There were also a radio
and telephone by the bed, several vases of flowers and the
decor was plain, fresh pale green and white, carpet,
curtains, bed spread all matching.

It had been another long day. Laurie was tired. They
had flown to Schiphol International Airport on a late
flight and she was ready for a hot bath and sleep. The
snack on the plane had been unwanted food and she was
not hungry. Ben had spent the flight working, his
briefcase open on his lap. She almost remarked aloud why
wasn't his briefcase attached to him permanently like a
kangeroo's pouch, but she did not feel he would
appreciate the crack.

She curled her arms round a pillow in the cool-sheeted
bed, and fell asleep dreaming of Ben, a faint smile on her
face. She was determined to enjoy these few hours with
him, even though they were separated by so many floors
and thicknesses of brick and cement.

Laurie was up early, discovering an indoor pool in the
basement of the hotel and a friendly attendant who lent
her a black swimsuit. She changed quickly and pinned her
plait on top of her head. The swimsuit was for a slightly
larger person and the straps kept falling off Laurie's
slender shoulders, but she enjoyed swimming up and
down in the heated water. The exercise gave her an
enormous appetite and when Ben joined her in the sunny
terraced dining-room for breakfast, she was already
helping herself to cheese, cold meats, eggs and crisp rolls
from the buffet table.

'Good morning, Laurie,' he said formally. 'Did you
sleep well?'

'Like a top,' she said cheerfully.

He noted the wet tendrils on her neck. 'So you found the pool?'

'It's lovely,' she said, popping a sliver of cheese into her mouth. 'The water was beautiful, so warm. You should have come for a swim.' She chose a table by a window, away from the potted palms and hanging ferns. 'Shall we sit here? I don't want to risk insects dropping into my coffee. It smells too delicious.'

He smiled at her enthusiasm. She was in jeans again, but her best white pair with a pleated primrose yellow blouse that tied in a big knot at her midrift. Her hair was kept off her face with a wide yellow tennis style headband.

'I've been meaning to ask again why you sent Trudy to me. I know it's too much to expect that you suddenly think the Alexander Technique is the flavour of the month. And I'm sure you are far too professional to use a young girl as a human experiment—that would be too irresponsible for words.'

A calculating gleam came into his eyes. 'It was partially a challenge, I'll admit. I decided there was no risk to Trudy, whatever you did or did not do would be harmless. You haven't been able to give me any proof of any kind that your technique is beneficial.'

'It's incredibly complex,' said Laurie helplessly. 'I can't give you proof on a plate. I can recommend books to read, give you electromyography patterns to study, X-rays that show spinal changes. But there's no way of forcing results. It's as I keep telling Milly. I don't want her to care whether she's doing it right or wrong, because the moment she doesn't care, then the obstacle is gone.'

'I'm afraid it's all too complicated for a simple country doctor like myself,' he said with an exaggerated modesty that made Laurie want to shake him. 'I'd better stick to sutures and the prescription pad.'

'You don't want to know,' said Laurie, squirting runny egg yolk with an indignant jab of her spoon. 'Any new thought is a threat to your citadel, your precious medical fortress.'

'Flowers are no threat,' he said enigmatically.

'I don't follow . . .'

'It's your nick-name at Cumthwaite Hall. They call you Little Flower. You look like one this morning, all dewy.'

'You mean a cauliflower.'

'Like a daffodil,' he said, his eyes twinkling. He leaned back lazily, enjoying her discomforture. His casual friendliness was disarming. 'Or a crocus. I'm not very good on flowers either.'

'Some of the species are deadly.'

'I'm not used to breakfasting with any flower. So you'll be out sightseeing this morning?' he enquired, biting into his toast and marmalade.

'You bet. I don't intend to waste a minute.'

'I wish I was coming with you, but I'm otherwise occupied.' He sounded genuinely envious.

'I know. It's never too late to learn.'

'New techniques and discoveries. It's a useful pooling of information.'

'See you this afternoon with the other fish, then.'

'Watch out for the barracudas.'

Strolling along the elm-lined canals by the handsome seventeenth century burghers' houses, Laurie thought how unexpectedly nice the weekend was becoming. She let the dappled sunshine play on her face as she stopped to admired the tall, gabled houses, each one a different design and decoration to its neighbour.

She began to identify the four styles of gable, the step, the spout, the neck and the bell, then the cornice gable of the wider houses, heavy beams jutting out from the top that once hauled up cargoes. Half-way up many of the old houses were gablestones on which were carved the owner's name and occupation.

She had a wonderful morning, taking in a cruise in a glass-topped boat through the canals in the heart of the city. They glided passed the old merchants' warehouses, houseboats and floating markets. She saw the cats' houseboat where a Dutch cat lover cared for the city's strays. She saw the Weeper's Tower next to the old St Nicolaaskerk, Rembrandt's house in Jodenbreestraat, and lastly the home of Anne Frank.

She found this narrow house and the concealed room behind the bookcase unbearably moving. To think of the young girl and her family hidden in that small space during the German occupation and to see the children's drawings on the walls, the faded cut-outs from magazines still pinned up, Anne's diary preserved in the museum. It reminded her of the cruelty still in the world.

The morning sped past. There wasn't time for the famous Rijksmuseum or the new modern one devoted entirely to Van Gogh, or to stop and listen to the music of a street organ. She had a quick snack of a hearty *broodje* sandwich filled with smoked fish and salad and a cup of deliciously creamy coffee.

She pinned on a conference badge and hurried to make the Conference Hall by two o'clock. The big octagonal hall was already full of delegates and Laurie squeezed in at the back, merging with the crowd, being inconspicuous. Ben was already on the podium in the centre of the wide stage, looking tall and splendid, not in a formal suit as she had expected, but casual in his suede jacket with a dark shirt and trousers.

Laurie was on the edge of her seat as he was introduced by the President of the Conference. Ben's list of credentials was long and awesome. He listened, as he probably had many times before, his face impassive.

Professor Ben Vaughan began his lecture. His subject was the phenothiazines, the most important group of major tranquillizers. His voice rich and deep, he was authorative and forceful but there was an underlying modesty in the way he put over the facts as if he had come by them almost by accident. He was relaxed, using the whole stage to walk about, occasionally leaning against the sidearches, loosening the knot of his silk tie as the room became too warm. He had humour too, coming down to the front row of his audience to find a guinea-pig to demonstrate some point.

He hardly used his notes, only referring to them for statistics or dates. Delegates hung on every word, some wearing head-sets linked to the interpreters. Laurie almost burst with pride. She was so proud of him, of his knowledge, of his skill in communication. He had a powerful delivery and passionate belief in his message.

If only she was the wife of this utterly masculine man, her pride in him would be complete. But who was she? No one really, a teacher of a form of alternative medicine, a failed junior sister.

She looked round the hall, spotting several attractive women in the audience, his equal in status and knowledge. Any one of them would make the perfect Mrs Vaughan, a professor's wife. But perhaps he had eyes only for Priscilla, the lovely artist. Perhaps he needed someone who could take his mind off his work, and he had so much in common with Priscilla, especially their love of the Lake District.

Laurie twisted the knife expertly in her heart. She was very good at making herself suffer. She ruthlessly pushed the thoughts away, concentrating on the last minutes of Ben's lecture, realising just how important his influence could be for the future of prescribed drugs and patient care. She remembered times on the ward when she too had begun to wonder if some of the drugs weren't the cause of half the problems.

The applause broke out, loud and enthusiastic. Laurie was jerked back to the present, joining in the clapping, her face glowing with admiration. There was a healthy buzz of conversation as the delegates began to discuss points among themselves. Laurie felt out of it, not for the first time, but happy that it had gone so well.

Ben was surrounded by a press of people but it was easy to see his dark head above everyone. He was making slow progress through the crowd, so many people wanted to stop and talk to him. Laurie felt blissfully trapped as he found a gap and strode with purpose in her direction. He stopped in front of her, looking boyish and fractionally embarrassed by all the adulation. His forehead was shiny with the heat, his hair tousled.

'Did you fall asleep this time?' he asked.

A joke came quickly to her lips but she couldn't say it. She was loving him too much. 'You were wonderful,' she said, not caring how much he read into those words. 'I thought you were marvellous.'

'Steady on,' he said. 'That could got to my head.' But he looked pleased and took her arm possessively. She did not mind. He could hold her as much as he pleased. Several people looked in their direction. 'Let's celebrate our newly found amicability. How about dinner tonight? I'll take you out on the town.'

Laurie nodded. She did not know if she could keep her head on such a slippery slope. She must keep him at a distance, even if every bone in her body was melting towards him. She knew she had to be two women with separate identities, one who loved him, one who kept away from everything he stood for.

* * * * *

Their evening together began with drinks in a brown bar with Ben said she must see. They were atmospheric places, smoky and brown, oak beamed and full of the character of the solid Dutch. Then they moved on to a famous restaurant converted from five lopsided old houses alongside a canal. It was full of antiques and brasses and pictures of old Amsterdam.

'Dutch food is plain and hearty,' Ben said. 'But their sea food is excellent.' They started their meal with a dish of mussels and herring in a sauce that they both found delicious, followed by a traditional casserole which Ben would only translate as hunting stew, finishing with waffles and *slagroom*, whipped cream.

'What an odd word for something so nice,' said Laurie.

Ben noticed that she did not eat much but just tasted the dishes. 'Tomorrow night we'll eat Indonesian. It's lighter and really delicious.'

'Tomorrow?' She hardly dare repeat the word.

'You say that as if you did not believe tomorrow existed. But it does. It always comes. You have to believe that or there wouldn't be any point in all that we do.'

He was wearing a formal shirt and tie with his dark trousers and suede jacket, but he had loosened the tie in a casual manner. Laurie was disturbed by the sight of his strong neck, knowing how close the dark curls lay to that bold throat.

She was aware of her kindling senses, how much she was enjoying his company and enlivening conversation, how the warmth and cosiness of the restaurant were isolating them in a pool of intimacy. She was trying hard to forget how his hard body had felt against her own, yet everything about him, his craggy face, the tangy aftershave, the clever skilful hands, were reminding her fiercely of what she wanted.

'Oh tomorrow,' she said flippantly. 'It's just a word.

All that exists is the present.'

'And the past? Doesn't that influence the present?'

Laurie shuddered. 'S-sometimes . . .' Tears came unbidden into her eyes and she saw a look of concern cross Ben's face. He took her hand across the table.

'I'm sorry. Have I said something painful? Reminded you of something you're trying to forget.'

'It's nothing. You were suggesting Indonesian food. That's sounds lovely. I've never tried it before. I suppose it's sort of half-way between Chinese and Indian.' She was babbling on, trying to cover her moment of weakness. She stirred her coffee intently, staring into its rich depths. 'We shall still be here in Amsterdam, tomorrow?'

'Of course. I shall be free after lunch. We'll go sightseeing. We could hire a car, drive out into the countryside, look for a cheese market, find the bulb fields.'

'I'd like that.'

She was wearing her blue silk dress with her hair loose and free down her back. Two golden combs kept her hair swept back from her face, and her thick fringed lashes were touched with navy mascara. She looked so pretty and delicate that Ben found himself almost in awe of her. He felt huge and clumsy in her presence, like a giant in a fairy tale. But he was a good host anxious to put his guest at ease, to make her happy.

'Would you like to go to a nightclub?' Ben asked, after their second cup of coffee. 'Do you feel like dancing?'

'Do I feel like dancing?' she laughed. 'I always feel like dancing! When did I last dance? It must have been a million years ago.'

She hardly remembered the nightclub where Ben took her. It was somewhere below ground, under a bridge, where they almost had to fight to find a table. But the music was good. Ben had known that a striptease floor show would have offended her, and there was nothing more outrageous than old silent films thrown on to the whitewashed walls to remind the dancers that time passes and nothing lasts.

She should have known that he could dance. Disco or closely entwined together, his arms and feet knew what to do. Laurie was spinning in a world of enchantment, close in his arms, his scent, his body against hers, everything was magic and wonderful. In the pounding beat, there was no opportunity for intimate talk, but when the music slowed, his arms said everything, his face against her hair. These were secret moments, as precious as pearls, expressions of love and tenderness that reduced her to an aching softness. She linked her hands behind his dark head, fingers in the short curls at the nape of his neck, hoping she would never have to let go.

But even they tired of the heavy rock, and at some point he propelled her out into the cool night air, towards a taxi hat took them back to their hotel. He must have felt the same way, not wanting the evening to end, for he suggested a swim in the hotel pool.

'I've only a borrowed swimsuit,' she said.

'It's only a borrowed pool.'

The pool was deserted. The attendant had long gone home. The water was as still and blue as a lagoon. The surface broke into waves and ripples as Laurie plunged in, disturbing the silence.

Ben joined her and she had to avert her eyes from his splendid back and the breadth of his brown shoulders. They swam and raced, diving below the surface, seeing the other in a wavering silhouette, hands gliding across silky skin, arms and legs entwining below the water.

'Laurie darling,' he breathed, pulling her towards him. 'My little water-nymph. You are so beautiful.'

She felt his hands move down her spine, pinning her hips against his thighs. She could hear her heart hammering but there was simply no stopping him. All the desires of her hungry body were awakened and could not be stilled.

'Did you think at all about what I said this morning at breakfast?' said Laurie desperately, saying anything to still the tumult in her heart. 'About before your lecture?'

'I wondered when you were going to ask me,' he said tormenting her with brief sweet kisses down her slender neck. 'I did give it some thought, but not much. You could hardly expect me to pick up a new mental technique without the benefit of expert tuition.'

'No, of course not, I didn't expect . . .' She arched her back in delicious anticipation as his hands slid silkily over her waist and down the sides of her thighs. Her body was turning to molten fire and she was surprised that the water was not bubbling around her skin.

'But I did try to keep my mind clear and in focus,' he said in such tender tones that Laurie wondered what she had done to deserve them. 'Everytime a worrying thought nagged me about the lecture, I mentally took myself aside. Look, I said, the lecture is not till two o'clock so quit worrying till five to.'

'And did it work?' Laurie murmured against his mouth.

'It seemed to. I had a very . . . useful morning,' he breathed, tracing the line of her hair round the shells of her ears. He nibbled the soft lobes with delicious nips.

Laurie closed her eyes with a secret, elated smile. This was no time for chipping away at defences of his mind when his hands were bringing her body to life. His demanding mouth was opening her lips, his tongue exploring the warm moist tissue inside, intimately clamouring for her flesh with a hunger she had never expected.

She clung to him as if there was no outside world and there was nothing but his firm mouth on hers, and his arms welding her to him. Her body was a raging inferno, despite the cool water, and she could only go along with the storm of desire flooding in her veins. Her fingers raked through the dark hair on his chest, searching for the feel of the hardness of his flesh. The straps of the swimsuit slipped off her wet shoulders, and with a groan he nuzzled deeply into her soft breasts, tasting the moist sweetness and filling his mouth with her hardened nipples.

Suddenly there were other faces, other voices in her head, cruel and mocking . . . her thoughts swam in utter confusion.

'Here's a nice little nursie. Very nice indeed. I don't think this one's had it before! Been let down by some man, ducky?'

Laurie panicked. She cried out, taking in great gasps of breath as she struggled, fighting him off. She could not think straight, only that a man, some strange man, someone stronger than herself, was intent on invading her body.

'Don't! Don't touch me! Leave me alone . . .'

'Laurie, what's the matter? Laurie, don't fight me . . . I won't hurt you.'

'No, go away. I can't, I can't . . .'

His body gleamed from the water, muscles so strong. Laurie was terrified. She struggled like a creature possessed.

'Laurie darling, don't be afraid. Look, I won't touch you. I'll stand back.'

'Go away, all of you,' she sobbed. 'You ought to be ashamed of yourselves . . .'

Ben tried to calm her, pushing back the hair from her distraught face. 'Hush, hush, there's no one else here. Don't cry, darling. Don't cry.'

The gremlins flooded into her mind, the pool echoing with sounds till she could no longer hear Ben. Rasping, strident voices grated in her head, making the raw nerve ends tingle with pain. The water slapping against the sides became footsteps running on the tiled floor of Casualty. She shut her eyes, unable to stand the glare of the bare electric bulbs as they began to swing erratically from the ceiling.

Her fingers dragged the swimsuit straps back on to her shivering shoulders, their tips remembering the feel of broken buttons and snapped thread. She wanted to cover the nakedness with her torn uniform, but only water slid through her fingers.

Frantically she tried to get away but Ben seemed to be everywhere blocking her escape. As she thrashed about, a heavy wet rope of hair whipped across her face like a slap. Shocked, her voice stuck in her throat; she could not speak a word.

'It's your hair, only your hair, Laurie,' said Ben, catching her flailing arms. 'Let's take you out of the water. Come on, sweetheart. You're very tired. Let's find the steps.'

She was tired—she was conscious of a tremendous tiredness. What had made her so tired? It was as if the exhaustion had been dormant for years, waiting to surface with a debilitating force that made her head spin weakly.

'Get away,' she moaned, giving him a sudden push.

With a cry of anguish, she was free, floundering through the water to the sides, and climbing out of the pool. She could not look back, but she heard the angry splash of his arms as Ben ploughed to the end of the pool in a furious crawl.

Shivering, Laurie wrapped a towel round her and clutching her clothes, ran through the deserted corridors and up the stairs to the safety of her room. She could hardly breath.

She staggered into the bathroom and pulled off the swimsuit, still shaking with fear. It was no good; she would never be able to love a man fully. Her mind was warped and irrevocably scarred. She would always hear those voices. That night, three years ago, had robbed her of the ability to love.

The next morning she packed her bag and took a taxi to the airport. She talked the airline official into changing her flight booking, and before midday she was high over the Channel on her way back to Manchester.

The flight, the train ride, the rattling bus were a blur of movement and passing grey scenery. It was a nightmare that she somehow survived.

When she got back to Cumthwaite Hall, she was still in a daze. Faith saw her stricken face, but said nothing beyond a brief hello. Laurie hurried upstairs to her flat and collapsed on the bed, burying her face into the pillow, trying to quieten her shattering tears.

She could never be free of the past, and free to give her love to a man. There would always be shadowy figures behind her lover, reminding her of her own failure.

In the following weeks Laurie put her heart and soul into work, pushing herself until she was bone weary every evening. She took on extra students, gave free tuition, concentrated until her head ached. But the results were good—people appreciated her integrity and came back for more. Even young Trudy was infected with her enthusiasm and was willing to come twice a week for lessons. Now that she had her little car back on the road, Laurie made regular visits to Milly, checking her blood pressure and making sure there were no more fainting fits.

'You are so kind,' said Milly, as Laurie arrived at the cottage with a load of shopping from Windermere. 'I

can't get out so easily these days and my cats are too spoilt
to go hunting for themselves.'

'I think you feed them better than you feed yourself,'
said Laurie, stroking the nearest mobile bundle of soft
fur. 'It's tinned salmon and cold chicken for the pussies,
and bread and jam for you.'

'Oh dear,' said Milly mildly. 'Is that a reprimand,
Laurie? I keep forgetting you're a teacher. I'd better have
an egg then. Would you like a boiled egg, dear?'

Laurie smiled. 'Two boiled eggs coming up. You lay
the table and I'll make supper. Then we'll do a little work.
Have you been keeping up your semi-supine?'

'On and off. It's easy to forget. I do try.'

'I know. It requires self-discipline, every day. Come
on, you spoilt pussies. I've bought you some ox liver.'

She tried to find new interests for herself, accepting
invitations to visit Tasmin's home, to climb Skiddaw with
James and Faith, to wander the fells on her own and
explore the lakeside. She saw Ben once. She was in her
car, slowing down at a pedestrian crossing, when she saw
Ben coming out of a Windermere shop. He was carrying
an awkward, cumbersome package wrapped in brown
paper. Her foot went down on the brake pedal with a jolt.
Just that unexpected glimpse of him, his easy loose-
limbed ruggedness, threw her. He looked tanned. He was
followed by Priscilla, a vision in a casual pale yellow
trouser suit, the colour of meadow cowslips. She was
laughing at Ben's efforts to get the package into the back
of his car.

Laurie drove away, crashing the gears, tears almost
blinding her.

Olive kept her in touch with all the news. Laurie found
it difficult to discourage her. It seemed that Olive went to
the Boathouse twice a week to give it a good clean, so she
knew everything that was going on.

'Been away again, he has, to some South American Conference,' she told Laurie. 'Brazil of all places. Rio de Janeiro. And Miss Priscilla went with him. She wanted to paint the mountains and jungle, or whatever they have there. I suppose she's done all the Lake District by now and is looking for something new to get her teeth into!'

Or someone like Ben, thought Laurie uncharitably. 'That's nice for her.'

'They are such old friends, you know. They've known each other since they were children.'

'So you've told me before.'

'She's such a lovely girl, all that silvery hair.'

'Not a girl any more, surely? You've lost track of time, Olive. She must be forty if she's a day.'

Olive cleaned over the kitchen surfaces with a fast swipe. 'Never! Priscilla doesn't change. She'll always be young. She's that kind of person.'

Laurie shrugged. 'Some people have all the luck. Talent, beauty, immunity to ageing.' And Ben Vaughan, she added silently. It was not fair. Then she recalled that she did not want Ben either, so perhaps it was fair. She shook her head in bewilderment. These last days had been hard and her resolve to remain calm and distant was eroded by Olive's gossiping.

Sad rages of jealousy stirred in her heart. She knew it was pathetic—she had always despised jealousy and jealous people. It was a festering disease that tainted both sufferer and victim and she wanted nothing to do with it. But it seemed she had no control over her feelings, and the green heat was there despite her resolve to remain free of it.

She tried not to show the strain but Faith knew there was something wrong. She began to lighten Laurie's work load but Laurie did not want more free time. She wanted to be so busy that there was no time to think, so that she

slept from weariness, so that her mind was too numb to
think. It was often impossible, especially if she heard
Ben's car leaving for the hospital, or returning in the early
morning. Then she lay, twisting and turning in a hot
jumble of sheets, longing to see him again, her body
racked with anguish.

It was while she was feeling so low, that Bruce
telephoned. At first she did not recognise his voice, and
thought he was perhaps a student on the course.

'Oh Bruce . . . I'm sorry. I didn't realise it was you. I
thought you were someone phoning for an appointment.
How are you? How nice to talk to you. How's everyone at
St Ranulph's?'

'Everything is just the same, everyone is working their
guts out. Nothing has changed. How about you? Got
tired of the Lake District yet and making people stand
straight?'

Laurie could hear the tightness in his voice so she did
not attempt to explain the Alexander Technique to him
yet again.

'It's the most beautiful place. Lovely lakes and craggy
hills. I love it. And the school is going well. I've quite a
number of private students now. It's very encouraging.'

'That's good,' said Bruce, but he did not sound
convinced. 'Easier than nursing, eh? Nice clothes, nice
hours, nice pay. All right for some.'

'Bruce, I'm not going to have an argument with you,
but I do assure you I am working hard. Okay, it's
different and I don't have night duty, and no messy
chores. But the aim is the same. I am helping people live a
healthier life.'

'Can I come up and see you?' he asked abruptly. 'I've
a long weekend due it would be great to see you. I've got a
car now and we could go out. This place is dead without
you, absolutely ghastly. I really miss you, Laurie, and

need you terribly. We've got a lot of time to make up. It would be wonderful to get together again.'

Laurie's head was swimming. She did not want Bruce back in her life, empty though it might be now, and she was not going to let him make her feel guilty. She was sorry for him; they were both going through the same torment. But Bruce was no replacement for Ben. She would rather live alone, have no one; she could not pretend that the young doctor was anything but a unwanted admirer she could do without.

She knew she had to tread carefully. 'Bruce, I gave you an invitation to come up any time, and I meant it. You're very welcome to come . . . as a friend. But there isn't anything between us and never has been. And you don't need me, you only think you need me. I'd be no good for you, Bruce, the way I am, the way I feel. I really have changed. You ought to find yourself a girl who genuinely cares about you. But it isn't me. If you can't accept that I'm not for you, then it would be better if we don't see each other.'

'How do you know what I need? You know I'm nuts about you, Laurie. We've always got on so well . . .' he began arguing loudly and Laurie held the phone away from her ear. She did not want to listen to a long rigmarole of how much he needed her. He was not concerned about her feelings, what she needed or what was best for her. Bruce was only thinking of himself.

'Look, Bruce, I've got to go. Please try to understand. I don't want you in my life if you're going to try and push me into a false situation. It would be nice to have you as a friend. A good friend. Nothing more. I've tried not to hurt you, but I can't say things I don't mean and never will.'

'But Laurie darling—'

'I'm not your darling.'

'You don't mean that. You can't.'

'Goodbye Bruce.'

She put the phone down, and leaned against the wall. letting Bruce's voice wash away. She never wanted to hear from him again. She hoped he would take some notice, and find himself another girl somewhere, anyone.

Olive came through from the kitchen, a wicker basket over her arm. Laurie looked at the basket hardly recognising it. It all seemed so long ago.

'Mr Ben just dropped by with this. He said you'd left it behind in his car. I told him you were on the phone to your boyfriend in London and he said not to bother you.'

Laurie took the basket and held it listlessly. It was dusty and stale, like herself. 'Thank you, Olive,' she said, her voice empty of emotion. 'I'd forgotten all about it.'

What did it matter if Ben believed she had a boyfriend tucked away somewhere. He had left her alone since Amsterdam. It would be safer if the rift widened to an uncrossable chasm.

CHAPTER NINE

IT WAS late August. Windermere was still bursting at the shores with holidaymakers; they swarmed everywhere, shopping, sailing, steaming, sunbathing, sandpie making. Children crying, parents arguing, shorts and burnt knees, sun tops and burnt shoulders.

Laurie enjoyed being among the crowds at Windermere and Bowness. The piers were packed with endless queues as a trip on a steamer up to Ambleside or south to Lakeside was a must for every holiday family.

'It's getting worse every year,' said Tasmin. 'All these people are spoiling the lakes.'

'But it's peaceful here,' said Laurie, stretching out her legs on the grass.

'Thank goodness for Cumthwaite Hall,' said Faith. 'Our own personal oasis.'

Laurie agreed, silently. She had come to terms with not seeing Ben. He was hardly around Cumthwaite Hall, spending all his time at the hospital or away lecturing and driving back through the night. It had rained for a week after their return from Amsterdam, and the greyness of the skies and blackness of the mountains had matched her mood. The waves on the lake forlorn and colourless, lapping against broken branches of trailing storm-torn trees and overhanging grasses. Laurie wandered for hours along the rainswept shore, reluctant to admit that she was worn out by indecision. She loved Ben, but she could never love him openly. Tears flooded her eyes as she saw a dim future without him, without anyone.

But as suddenly the clouds fled and the weather

improved, and with it, Laurie's spirits began to recover, slowly at first, a little damaged but basically intact. Her enthusiasm for the Alexander Technique and her work among the students gave her a much needed lifeline and she clung to it with tenacity, determined that loving Ben was not going to destroy her. She had suffered once from the cruelty of fate, and she would not allow it to happen a second time.

It did not go unnoticed. If Faith caught a sad expression on Laurie's face, she immediately found some excuse for a discussion on homeopathy or a student's condition and progress. Laurie was grateful for her silent sympathy but never confided. She did not know if Faith was aware that the cause of her depression was the difficult and prickly professor living in the Boathouse. His name was rarely mentioned, and then only in the context of the lease of Cumthwaite Hall which was still unresolved.

The long summer evenings were drawing in but as Laurie strolled in the parkland, she could hear music in the still air from one of the evening cruise boats. Sounds carried a long way over water—birds flocking to roost, geese honking in formation. She smiled to herself as she imagined people enjoying themselves, perhaps dancing on the deck, or just drinking while they listened to the music. Faint laughter joined the lapping water as Laurie neared the shore. Now she could see the lights of the cruising steamboat as it glided up the lake, and the shimmering reflections of brightness on the dark water.

The lights were confusing, and in the fading dusk Laurie could not make out which way the steamer was going. It seemed to be going in both directions which was impossible. She rubbed her eyes and blinked, wondering if the distortion was her own tired eyesight at fault.

In a shattering, heart-stopping second, she knew the

answer. She shouted a warning but her voice simply disappeared into a void. As she ran, distraught, the last few yards to the edge of the lake, she heard the ominous crunch of metal and wood as the two steamers collided sideways on. The sound of laughter turned immediately to cries and screams—terrifying sounds that sent cold shivers down Laurie's spine. All was a confusion of ripping wood, torn metal, hissing steam, and still the taped music played on.

Laurie stood transfixed, wringing her hands, her breath contorted. Someone had said something, somewhere, a warning about the danger of a collision on the crowded lake . . . the words spun round in her mind. She tried to marshall her thoughts. What should she do? Get help. Alert the emergency services. TELL SOMEONE.

She ran back to Cumthwaite Hall, staggering and stumbling over the uneven grass. She could hardly get the words out, a pain constricting her chest, as she found James and Faith in his office working on the accounts.

'James, an accident . . . on the lake, two steamers have collided. There are people in the water . . . phone the police, ambulances. I'm going back . . . Ben's boat . . . get to them.'

His face went pale, even his grizzly red beard seemed to lose colour. 'Oh my God,' he said, his hand going immediately to the phone. 'I knew it would happen one day.'

'Ben's friend . . . the artist, Priscilla,' Faith whispered, ashen. 'I think I saw her on the pier, waiting for the evening cruise. She was with a tall, dark man . . . I couldn't see who it was.'

Laurie hardly heard her. A tall dark man . . . oh no, not a tall, dark man. It couldn't be Ben, surely? But it could only be Ben with Priscilla. She felt a rush of despair clutch her heart, grief swelling her throat. She couldn't speak.

She ran around, automatically gathering first-aid equipment, sheets, towels, anything she could find that would be useful. James and Faith hurried out of Cumthwaite Hall with her, helping to carry the load. The sounds from the lake were awful, the cries and screams, splashing water. Out of the gloom came two figures, dripping and gasping, staggering towards the shore having swum the distance. Olive came from somewhere, hurrying with an armful of blankets, her face pinched with distress.

'Oh, this is dreadful. Miss Priscilla's on that steamer,' she cried. 'It's her birthday. They were going for a birthday cruise to Ambleside, just for fun, just for a laugh.'

'We'll find her,' said Laurie. 'Don't worry. We'll find her. She'll be all right.'

And Ben, she prayed. Please don't let Ben be hurt. Please don't let him be a hero, getting into danger, helping people. I want him safe.

James jumped into Ben's boat while Faith untied the mooring. They were both experienced sailors and knew what they were doing. Laurie stood by, helpless, wondering how she had expected to navigate on her own.

'You stay here,' James shouted. 'One less in the boat will make room for more survivors. You're more use on shore, Laurie. Olive, take anyone who can walk back to Cumthwaite Hall and make them comfortable. The ambulances should be arriving any minute.'

Laurie nodded. It made sense. She turned to Olive. 'Come and help me. Let's see what we can do.'

She tried to close her ears to the sounds coming from the crippled steamers and turned her attention to the two survivors scrambling ashore. The youths were not badly hurt, but shocked and shivering from the coldness of the water. She directed Olive to wrap blankets round them, and when they were capable of walking, to take them back to the hall. Out of the gloom came more figures. She sat them on the grass and bound cuts and gashes, talking in a calming, soothing voice as they gasped out their experiences.

'It was awful, awful . . . The steamers were just passing and we were waving, then suddenly the other one swerved right into us.'

'My family is out there, my wife, baby son . . . I couldn't find them. I don't know why I started to swim. I must go back!'

'Stay here,' said Laurie, restraining an anguished young man. 'You're bleeding badly, and you've lost a lot of blood. There are other people out there now with boats. They'll find your wife and son.'

Laurie had to forcibly keep him down. He was in no fit condition for a second immersion. She felt so sorry for him, having guilt to worry about as well.

'They are doing all they can,' she told an elderly man, very distressed because he had been separated from his wife. 'We'll watch the boat coming in. They'll find her, don't worry. I'm sure there will be more rescue services putting out from Bowness. I can hear their engines now.'

'I hope you're right. Emmie's not really very well. That's why we came away for a bit of a holiday. She had just gone to the ladies, or we would have been together . . .' he whispered, hiding his head in his trembling hands.

Laurie could do nothing more for him. He refused to go to the Hall, wanting to wait for the boat coming in. She made sure he was well-wrapped up in a blanket. Olive appeared again, this time with a hamper of hot drinks. Laurie left him being persuaded to drink some tea.

Ben, where are you, her inner voice called to him. Where are you when I want you? Please keep yourself safe, you are so valuable. Don't keep diving into the water till you're too exhausted to float—don't struggle against odds you can't win. Laurie knew her thoughts were totally selfish but she didn't care. No one mattered more than he. He was the most important person in her life.

She saw someone being brought ashore in Ben's boat and caught sight of a sheen of silver hair. But it wasn't Priscilla. It was a far older woman and she was in a bad way. With a sinking heart, Laurie wondered if was the old man's wife, Emmie. The woman was blue around the mouth and had a bad leg wound. Laurie stanched the blood, her hands automatically doing what was necessary.

'Emmie? Emmie?' she asked softly.

'Yes? My husband . . . have you seen my husband?'

'Yes, he's here. He'll be glad to see you.' But when were the ambulance men coming? They'd had long enough to get there. It seemed hours since the accident.

Laurie sat back on her heels, to take in a big breath. Her back was aching, her face damp with perspiration. She dried her hands on her hips and turned to the next shocked survivor.

Land Rovers were being driven from Cumthwaite Hall and their headlights turned on to illuminate the scene on the shore. Laurie could harldy believe the extent of the chaos and confusion. People floundering in the water; a flotilla of small boats bringing them ashore; residents from Cumthwaite Hall hurrying across the grass with more blankets and sheets. Every bed in the Hall must have been stripped.

Laurie hurried from group to group, assessing injuries, giving first-aid where possible, giving instructions for the care and removal of the more seriously injured. The fact that someone was in charge, knew what they were doing, was invaluable. And all the time, hidden from view, her heart was dying for want of news of Ben.

'Laurie . . . Miss Young . . .' A young girl was retching by the side of the lake. Laurie recognised the tangled mane of hair. It was Trudy, soaked and shivering, white with shock. Laurie supported her until the worst was over, and then wrapped a blanket round her, rubbing her hands. She was not hurt, only very shocked.

'My m-mum's in Ben's boat,' she stuttered. 'She's awfully hurt. She was leaning over the side when the steamers collided and fell on the rail. She's in a lot of p-pain . . .'

'Don't worry. We'll go and find her. Are you all right now?'

'I think so. The other steamer swerved, suddenly, trying to avoid a small sailing dinghy. There were a couple of lads in it and they didn't know what they were doing. They weren't looking where they were going. It looked like a moth on the water, and then it went down, its sails dragging . . . I couldn't see what happened to the people in it.' She began to cry again.

'Come along,' said Laurie. 'Let's go and see your mother. Can you walk?'

Laurie should have known. She should have known weeks ago. When she caught sight of a mass of silvery-blonde hair against Faith's shoulder, she realised that Priscilla was Trudy's mother. It would explain Ben's interest in Trudy, paying the bill for her lessons . . . it was all part of his strong attachment to the lovely artist. Laurie's heart felt as if it was being shredded but she hid her feelings as she went to tend the new load of injured passengers which James had just brought ashore. There was an elderly lady who had clearly had a heart attack after the disaster. There were small children bruised and frightened. Priscilla was clutching her ribs and clearly in a lot of pain.

'Mum . . . mum, are you all right?' cried Trudy, running to her side.

'Of course, darling,' Priscilla whispered, tentatively patting her daughter's shoulder though it was obvious even that small movement was painful.

Smashed ribs, possible internal injuries, thought Laurie, quickly separating mother and daughter, so that she could do something to make Priscilla more comfortable. She was trying to do a dozen things at once . . . the old lady, the children, Priscilla.

'We're going out again,' James called, revving the cruiser's engine.

Laurie flew around, thankful at last to see some ambulance men coming across the grass with stretchers.

'Thank goodness. At last. Where have you been?' she snapped, all nurse. 'These people over here need to be taken to a hospital quickly.'

'We got here as fast as we could, miss,' said one of the men, recognising authority. 'This is the back of beyond. We couldn't find the entrance.'

'Where's . . . where's my . . .?' Priscilla whispered, struggling against the pain of breathing, tears on her cheeks. 'Where is he? Someone please find him.'

Laurie nearly choked. How could she say that she had not seen Ben. She bound Priscilla's ribcage carefully, to give support. 'Don't try to talk,' she soothed. 'Take small, shallow breaths through your mouth.'

Laurie turned her attention to the old lady. Although Laurie had seen death many times, she never got used to it. The old lady was going. Laurie went down on her knees and held the cold hands gently, pausing for a few moments, not wanting to hurry the spirit away but let it depart in peace, in its own time. Even the trees seemed to stop rustling. Someone's mother, grandmother, grey hair plastered to a waxen forehead . . . Laurie closed the frail eyelids and moved away to the living.

A man was wading through the shallows, stumbling across from the shore, searching among the huddled groups. He was tall and dark, but slim as a reed and sinewy, torn wet clothes flapping in the wind. He fell on his knees beside Priscilla, put his arms round her and buried his head in her hair. In a moment, Trudy was hugging him too, and his arm drew her into his embrace. Laurie watched the small tableau, not quite understanding.

They were a family, complete, oblivious to the world. Priscilla, Trudy and who else? A tall, dark man who was helping the ambulance men put Priscilla on a stretcher and into a waiting ambulance. Laurie stared at him in the half light. He was like Ben, only he was not Ben.

'Would you help patch up this little one, Sister please,' said a deep, rough voice at her side. 'Cut knees and fright mostly.'

Ben was standing with a child in his arms. He was like a rescuer from the tales of old, a knight in armour, but instead of a heraldic breastplate or fine clothes he was wearing a dark dripping suit.

'Ben! You're safe. You're . . . not dead,' Laurie sobbed, flinging herself at him without thinking. He steadied her with one hand, protecting the child in his arms at the same time.

'Hold on, Laurie. Don't suffocate me. Mind the child.'

'I thought you were dead . . . I didn't know where you were.' She was helpless to stop the tears.

He felt the pulse beating in his wrist. 'Yes, you're quite right. Not dead. I'm still here.'

'Oh, don't joke,' she choked. 'I've been through agony, thinking you were dead, jumping in and out of the water saving people.'

He nodded. 'A hero's death,' he said, passing over the

little girl. 'Not for me. I haven't the courage. See to this youngster. I've got her mother down there under the beech tree. Bring her over as soon as you can. I've told the mother that the girl is all right, but she won't believe me till she sees her daughter herself.'

He tipped Laurie's face and looked into her tear-filled eyes. 'Cheer up. I'm here to fight you another day.'

Laurie couldn't speak. She was brimming with emotion, relief that he was all right; confusion that Trudy was Priscilla's daughter, perhaps even Ben's own daughter. How was she ever to know the truth?

A shiver crossed his broad shoulders and Laurie realised how wet he was. He was in a smooth barathea dinner jacket with braided lapels, a once sparkling white shirt now muddy and bloodied, a black string bow-tie half untied. He still looked marvellous, dark and saturine, smouldering with suppressed anger at the futility of the injuries.

'You're soaked,' she said. 'I'll get you some dry clothes.'

'You won't. You'll do nothing of the sort. You'll stay here and get on with your job. I won't die from a dip in the lake. And it isn't the middle of winter, thank goodness, or half these people wouldn't have been able to swim ashore. See to the child, then that woman in red who has a broken wrist. Can you strap it immobile before she goes to hospital to have it set?'

He was totally professional again, super-cool and serious, his face one of concern and concentration. Laurie put her mind to the injured and shocked survivors, but now with a new comfort in her heart. She knew that she loved him so much that she could bear it if he loved another. All she wanted was that he should be safe and well, and living and breathing in this world. That she might see him occasionally. If he really loved another, so be it. She would devote her life to her work and perhaps one day loving him would not hurt so much.

There were more helpers now. Doctors and nurses were arriving from the Westmoreland Infirmary and other hospitals and the pressure lifted from Laurie. She collapsed in a heap, suddenly every bone in her body protesting at the strain, her head aching. In the gloom, in the middle of the lake, she saw the outline of the two crippled vessels, one listing to starboard, the other fairly stable. They were surrounded by smaller boats, police rescue launches, a fire-boat. The situation seemed to be under control.

The first ambulances had already left taking the injured to hospital. Priscilla had given up her place in the queue because of Trudy. She was having a hard time persuading Trudy to stay at Cumthwaite Hall. She wanted to go with her mother.

'You can come and see me very soon,' said Priscilla, more calmly now. 'But there are other people who must go in the ambulance. You're not hurt, thank God. Stay here with Olive and be a good girl. Your father will take you home when there's transport. Please don't be difficult, Trudy.'

'I'll look after her,' said Olive. 'Drink this tea, love.'

'I don't like tea. I want to stay with my mum.'

'Drink it,' said Olive firmly.

It seemed like hours later that Laurie finally stopped working and the last of the injured were driven away. The shore line was littered with belonging, bags, hats, shoes, sunglasses. Wearily Laurie began to collect them up, putting them in a pile for identification.

'Let someone else do that, Laurie,' said Ben, rubbing the stiffness from his face. He was sitting on the grass, his arms straight behind him. 'You've done enough. Come away. There's nothing more you or I can do here. Let's go.'

'I must go back to Cumthwaite Hall. It's full of shocked people waiting to be taken home. They might need help.'

'There's half a dozen nurses from the Infirmary taking care of them, and Olive will be in her element organising everything. I'll just thank James and Faith and tell them that I'm taking you back to the Boathouse.'

Laurie didn't argue. She was too tired. She just let herself be ordered about. They stood in a group talking with James and Faith for a few minutes, voices hushed and tired, their faces wane in the harsh lights set up by the rescue services.

'You two have done a wonderful job,' said Ben. 'First on the scene. It made a lot of difference, stopping the panic, letting everyone see that help was coming. You must be worn out. Go home and make plenty of hot coffee and brandy. Hot baths and sleep. Look after yourselves now.'

'No, it was Laurie,' said Faith brokenly. 'She saw it. She came and got us. If it hadn't been for Laurie . . .' James had his arm round her and she leaned against him, looking drawn and older. The trauma of the night had taken its toll. Somewhere an owl hooted, dismal and forlorn.

'The authorities will have to do something now,' said James grimly. 'All that traffic on the lake. They can't ignore it now. I knew this would happen one day.'

'Something always has to happen before anyone will do anything about it,' said Faith incoherently.

They went away together, arms entwined, both shattered.

'Come along, Laurie,' said Ben firmly. 'No more work. You look a mess.'

'You don't exactly look a matinee idol yourself despite the posh dinner jacket,' she said, finding the spirit from somewhere. 'You're a bit overdressed for an evening cruise, aren't you?'

'What cruise?'

'Don't you have a date?'

'Had,' he corrected. 'It's probably all over now. A very stuffy academic dinner in Manchester. I was on my way when I realised something was happening on the lake. I must remember to phone up with my apologies, though they'll have heard about this on the news.'

He put his arm round her shoulders in a warm companionable way and turned her in the direction of the Boathouse.

'You weren't with Priscilla then?' she asked slowly. 'For her birthday?'

'Her birthday? Is it her birthday?' he sounded vague. 'Poor Priscilla. Some birthday it turned out to be. I'll phone the hospital and see how she is.'

'Don't you even know the birthday of the woman you love?' Laurie cried out, losing all control. 'That's wonderful. Some men are so thoughtless. Oh, I've no patience with you. Thank goodness you're not the man in my life.'

'Hold on, you scatty girl. What's this all about? The woman I love . . . how do you know who I love? Have you some special insight? Have I ever told you?' His eyes were glinting in the darkness, and she felt his grip tighten on her arm.

'I don't have to be told,' she said defiantly. 'I know it's Priscilla. I've got eyes, haven't I? You're head over heels in love with her and I'm not surprised. She's beautiful, sweet-natured, talented . . .' Laurie piled on the agony. It was a relief to get it into the open.

'This sounds like a Priscilla fan club eulogy. Do I love Priscilla?' he was asking himself in a detached manner. 'Yes, I suppose I do. I've never really thought about it before. I certainly loved her at age seven when she was an adorable and haughty thirteen-year-old with braces on her teeth. Yes, Laurie, with your unfailing instinct for hitting the nail on the head, you have made me realise a secret and unswerving love.'

He was making fun of her. It took her breath away. She did not know what to think.

'But she's married,' Laurie protested, dredging up her newest piece of information.

'So? She's married to Geoffrey, a really nice chap. They've been married for fifteen years. He's an architect. A perfect match in every way.'

'Trudy's fifteen, isn't she?'

'Ah, these artists, Laurie . . .' he said solemnly. 'They lived together before they were married. Very daring for those days.'

As they reached the sturdy Boathouse, Laurie's head was swimming. The waves lapping against the timbers reminded her of the cold lake waters. Perhaps Priscilla was not the love of his life after all. His words were not those of a lover, or someone who was having an affair. Had she got it all wrong after all? She was really too tired to think now. It would all have to wait till the morrow.

Her pretty coral track suit was ruined. The stains would never wash out, especially the grass stains. Still it was a small price to pay. Some people would never fully recover from the accident. Their lives would be completely changed.

'You can have the bathroom first,' said Ben, opening the door to the Boathouse. 'But be quick, or I warn you, I'll jump in too.'

'But you're the one who's all wet,' she objected.

'Don't argue, woman,' he said, pushing her upstairs. 'You're all in. Help yourself to something to wear.'

'You're always offering me your clothes.'

'I take that as a very good omen,' he said without

expression. But there was something deep in his eyes that turned her limbs to water. He took her fingers and kissed them, one by one, the sharp edge of his teeth teasing the soft pad of her thumb.

'Laurie,' he said. 'Please don't run away again. We have so much to talk about. This time, we must talk. Whatever happens between us, if there's to be any kind of future, we must talk.'

CHAPTER TEN

LAURIE lowered herself carefully into the tub of hot water, still shaken by the touch of his lips. Her naked shoulders shivered as she watched a drift of high clouds float across the silvery moon, silhouetted in the circle of the porthole shaped window. Could Ben blot out the years of anguish she had suffered, a man with wonderful hands and fire in his veins? She did not even dare wonder what she was doing here, with him, or allow herself another failure.

She sank deeper into the water, splashing it over her skin letting the heat soothe aching muscles. A nurse's paradise after long duty on a ward . . . it was always bliss. She pulled herself up sharply. One evening ministering and she was thinking like a nurse again. She hurried out of the masculine lobelia-blue bathroom, wrapped in an outsize towel, steaming and glowing and dripping. Ben was in his bedroom, searching for clothes. She averted her eyes from his bare, hairy legs and bare feet beneath the brief towelling robe. He had nice feet, broad and firm. She would have kissed them in her dreams. Those silly dreams.

He gave a short laugh. 'Look at my bed!' he said. 'Olive has been up here. She hasn't even left me a pillowcase.'

It was true. His bunk had been completely stripped of its covers. He was rummaging through a mahogany chest of drawers and tossed Laurie a pair of poppy red silk pyjamas still in their cellophane wrapping.

'You'd better get some clothes on,' he warned, his eyes

darkening as he took in her glistening skin. 'Would you like these?' he asked.' 'Not my style. I've never worn them.'

'A present from Priscilla?'

'No. I won them in a hospital raffle if you must know.'

He peeled off the towelling robe, his back to her, and stepped into the bathroom. It was done without embarrassment and Laurie could only marvel at the perfection of his back and narrow hips. How she longed to put her arms round him and feel that smooth skin against her breasts. They tingled even at the thought of his nearness. She heard Ben turn on the shower and imagined him standing there under the sparkling waterfall, each inch of his skin so desirous. She shut the door to the bathroom, clutching the pyjamas.

Her stomach muscles tightened as the sensuous fabric moved against her skin. She did look good in the glamorous red silk. The pyjamas were far too large for her, but clinging in all the right places. She unplaited her hair, letting it swing round her shoulders to dry. Everywhere was so quiet, no more water, she could hear her own ragged breathing.

'If you are going to look like that, I can't vouch for what will happen,' said Ben from the doorway, damp and steaming, now clad in jeans and jersey, his dark eyes raking over her. 'Or will you rush away like a frightened rabbit? What is it, Laurie? What is it about me that you can't stand?'

'It isn't you,' she mumbled, not looking at him.

'Can't you cope with someone loving you? I suppose it's too strong an emotion. Does everyone and everything have to be cool and antiseptic? Is that the level of your feelings?'

Laurie's fingers trembled as she tried to fasten the last button. He came over and did it for her, his fingers brushing lightly against her skin. His brief touch transfixed her to the spot.

'Loving me?' she repeated indignantly, wondering if she had heard right. 'Did you say . . . loving me? Who is this mythical someone?'

He came back and folded his arms round her as if he never wanted to let her go. He planted his chin firmly on the top of her head, savouring the soft silkiness of her hair so close and sweet.

'Come off your high horse, Laurie. Loving you, darling girl. That's exactly what I said. Me loving you. I love you, though God only knows why when all we do is argue and fight. And you are most awkward female I've ever come across, but somehow you've got under my skin and that's where I want you to stay. All I want to do is to make love to you and take care of you. I want to rescue you every time you're stranded, help all your lame ducks, solve all those dreadful problems buzzing around in your pretty head. When you tell me what they are, of course. And if you ever do.'

'I don't believe this,' she said, trying to still the great surge of happiness racing through her. 'You can't mean it.'

'Do I say things I don't mean? How many times shall I tell you? I love you, I love you. And we'll sort out those problems, whatever they are.'

'Problems . . .' Laurie brooded, hardly hearing him, but allowing herself to lean against him. His words sounded like one of her dreams, impossible. 'They are insoluble. And I'm never going to tell anyone.'

'Don't be unfair to me, Laurie, I want to know why you won't let yourself be a woman, let yourself be loved by me. You were meant to know love, to be part of a real loving partnership. What is it that makes you act this way? I want to know.'

She threw her arms round his neck and pulled his face down to hers, laying her cheek against his, breathing him in, allowing herself this luxury, this one moment of pure happiness.

'No one can help me,' whispered Laurie in despair. 'It's no good. I'm never going to change. You'd better forget me. Go away and find someone else.'

'You should know me by now,' he said darkly, moving his hand slowly down her back, sending shivers along her spine. 'I'm as stubborn and awkward as you. I never give up.'

Ben led her down the spiral stairway and made her sit on the long sofa while he went into the kitchen. Laurie stared into the flickering flames, hating all the thoughts that were crowding into her mind. She couldn't tell him. How could she? She had to leave something of his feeling for her intact. It would be better if he did not know. He came back with two mugs of steaming coffee laced generously with brandy from a decanter.

'You need a little inner warmth,' he said as Laurie opened her mouth to protest. 'Something to thaw you out. And I want you to talk to me, even if I have to ply you with alcohol. We need to talk, Laurie. Please try. It's so important.'

Laurie sipped the fiery drink obediently, determined that nothing would make her change her mind, but gasping as the secondary impact of the brandy slipped down her throat. Ben lay back on the sofa, hands clasped round the mug, never taking his eyes from her, willing her to pull down the barrier between them.

'There's nothing to say. Please leave me alone, Ben. It's no good trying to make me talk. I don't want to tell you. It all happened a long time ago. There's nothing really.'

'All right,' he said casually. 'Tell me about nothing.

Nothing is my favourite topic of conversation right now. I'd like to hear all about nothing.'

A strange thing was happening inside her. It was like a glacier cracking, breaking up, retreating. The deep-frozen recesses of her mind were being eroded, shifting a few centimetres this way and that. It was as dramatic as the great volcanic eruptions and earth movements which had formed the wild and barren landscapes of Cumbria.

The splintering ice shocked her, sent a shudder through her slim body. It was not the alcohol. She had drunk brandy before. It was something more fundamental. Something that had been waiting for the right moment. Ben did not touch her, but stayed still, watching and observing. He knew instinctively that she was about to relive some dreadful memory, that he could only help by being there and keeping still.

'I trained at St Ranulph's,' she began, hesitatingly, her thoughts swimming through a jumble of half-remembered sensations. She was hardly aware of what she was saying, but it would not hurt to tell him that. It wasn't herself speaking at all, some stranger was talking. 'I always wanted to be a nurse, even as a little girl. Always bandaging my dolls or the cat. Poor thing, he spent most of his days trying to get out of rolls of inexpert bandaging.'

He took her hand gently and stroked the back. 'Poor cat.'

'He never bit me and he did love me, so it can't have been that bad. I had to work hard at St Ranulph's and study all hours for my exams. I didn't have parents in the background for support, only an exhausted aunt. I don't have to tell you about burning the midnight oil. It was the same for you, I suppose. But it was worth it, wasn't it? Nursing was my life.'

He let her pause while she drank some more of the

laced coffee. She was relaxing, some of the tenseness leaving
her body. Laurie could not believe this was happening, but
she loved him so desperately. it came to her in a blinding
flash that if she was to stay sane, he had to know, even if he
rejected her.

'What happened to change that?'

'Nothing. Nothing at all.'

'No, Laurie. That's not true. Something must have
happened.'

Laurie's hair fell forward so that it hid her face. He could
not see the torment in her eyes. How could she tell him? She
wanted to disappear into the walls. He would hate her for
ever more if he knew.

'You know what Saturday nights are like in Casualty
. . .' her voice was so low, he could hardly hear the words.
He bent closer, but not too close.

'It was worse than usual. There were drunks, of course,
and road accident cases after the pubs were let out. We were
used to all that. We could cope with the odd difficult drunk,
sober him up in a cubicle with black coffee.'

'I know. Not an easy duty. I've had to deal with a good
many drunks in my time.'

She was trembling. The hand limply in his grasp was
shaking like a fluttering leaf. 'There were dozens of them,
that particular Saturday, falling about all over the place.
There had been a big football match and the supporters had
been drinking and fighting, breaking windows and
overturning cars. We were busy patching up cut heads and
black eyes when . . . when . . . these thugs came in,
swaggering and shouting, brandishing knives and broken
bottles. They were some kind of gang, hooligans rigged up
with masks on their faces.'

Laurie could not go on. She hid her face in her hands,
the memories too vivid to voice. Ben let her weep, the warm
tears washing away some of the immediate distress till she

was ready to continue.

'Go on, Laurie. Tell me, just as it happened.'

'I don't remember what they called themselves. They were bikers, a lodge or something, I think. They came in and started wrecking the place, overturning trollies, pulling down curtains, smashing light bulbs. I've never been so frightened in all my life. People were shouting and screaming. The young doctors were helpless to regain order. What could they do? I was . . . I was . . .' her voice faltered. Ben did not move. She had to talk this out herself. 'I was in a cubicle with a woman who had been in a car accident. She was not too badly hurt, but I was taking fragments of metal out of her forearm. We tried to keep very quiet and still, not to attract attention, hoping the gang would go away.'

Laurie stopped. Her heart was beating like a wild thing. She could see everything again, so vividly, the moment when the cubicle curtains were whipped down and the gang of mindless thugs stood there.

'They came in, the hooligans, into the cubicle. One of them . . . I remember he had orange hair, a horried dirty colour, dyed and all spikey, big shoulders in a greasy shirt. He stood looking at me, gloating and greedy. He said something, something about "this is one who hasn't had it lately" and they all sniggered and laughed. He swaggered up to me and put his hands right on me. Then they were all around me, pushing and shoving. They pulled off my cap and tore off my apron . . . they were like beasts . . .'

Laurie buried her face in her hands, sobbing. Great wrenching sobs tore at her heart. Ben turned her towards him so that he could take her gently, carefully into his arms, and she let him hold her, soothing her till the worst of the storm of crying was over. Her hair tumbled over her shoulders and her eyes were swimming with tears.

'No more,' said Ben, his voice grim. 'That's enough. I don't want to hear any more, Laurie. It doesn't make any difference.' His face was gaunt, but he still held her and loved her and wanted more than anything in the world to erase those dreadful memories.

'But there's more. Much more. I have tell you now,' she hiccuped. 'That wasn't the end. There was worse to come. I was . . . was pushed on the floor, and I was fighting them off. It was all blurred faces and hot beery breath. I seemed to have strength from somewhere. But the leader, the orange one . . . he was so strong and so heavy . . . I thought I would have to give in. I was almost passing out, suffocating. Then someone else came into the cubicle. It was a probationer nurse. She was a sweet little thing, just eighteen, slim, waif-like, innocent . . .'

Her voice faltered. There was a long pause as her breath came in a great tortured gasp.

'They went for her. Instead of me. She didn't stand a chance.'

Ben thought for a moment that Laurie was going to die in his arms. Her cry was primeval, a high, agonised scream of women from centuries long gone. It had always happened. It was the price women paid simply for being women. It shattered every fibre of his being, shook him as nothing had ever touched him before.

'I didn't help. I didn't do anything. I just sat on the floor, useless and beaten,' Laurie was hysterical now. 'I let it happen. To this young girl, this little thing in my keeping. I was in charge. She was my responsibility but when it came to the crunch, I let her down. I just let it happen . . .' She wept against his shoulder, long draughts of tears. 'I would rather have died than have this on my conscience . . .'

He stroked her hair gently, letting the agony of it all come and wash through her. What could he say? He was a man. But just as helpless. How could he ease her memories?

'There were others around,' he said slowly, choosing his words carefully. 'Doctors, porters. Others in authority. You weren't the only one. You had a patient to think of . . . she must have been terrified too. Don't be so hard on yourself. There was a limit to your strength. What more could you have done? You did everything possible. Don't feel guilty . . .'

'But I am guilty. I feel guilty that I survived!' She almost shouted the words at him. 'It should have been me, not her. I should have been their victim, not that poor child. She was so young, so innocent. It was a desecration of her sweetness.'

Ben was torn with emotions of anger and impotence, fury at his own sex. What could he do to heal the woman he loved? He drew on all his store of patience and understanding.

'First, we will find out what has happened to her, Laurie' he said firmly. 'Tell me her name and I'll make some enquiries.'

'Amy . . . Amy Newman.' It was the first time she had said the name out loud.

'Did they catch the thugs?'

'Yes.'

'Did you have to give evidence?'

'Yes.'

He poured her some more coffee, stroking her hair back from her tear-stained face, saying no more. They would not talk about it again. Her soft beauty was ravaged by her crying but it did not stop him loving her. The past was over—the future had to be the healing.

'Stay here and try to relax while I make some phone calls. Rest awhile. Cry some more if you want to. It can't hurt to cry.'

'Do you hate me?' she whispered, looking up at him. 'Knowing this? Knowing why I can never love anyone?'

'Hate you?' He fell on his knees beside her, taking her hands and pressing them fervently against his face. 'Darling Laurie, how could I, when I love you so much? I hate myself, for not realising, for not understanding, for not being able to help you. I should have known. I'm a doctor and I didn't see the symptoms. I was blind. You make me feel very humble. I've never had anything so difficult to cope with in all my life, but I swear to you, that from now on, I'm going to spend every hour making living worthwhile for you.'

She touched the long side-burns that softened his hard jaw line. 'You don't know how happy that makes me,' she said softly. 'I thought you would hate me.'

'Never. I love you. I told you that.'

Her heart overflowed with love for him and she gripped him tightly, kissing his face again and again. 'And I love you, love you, love . . . truly, I love you.'

She felt curiously light and free of shame. Her heart was opening slowly, a kind of late flowering. Ben still loved her, despite all she had told him, and that was a miracle. She could hear him telephoning at the big desk by the window. One of Priscilla's paintings hung near it, a dramatic view of Skiddaw, wreathed in a luminous grey mist. Laurie could accept it now as a painting, not a person.

The sound of his voice, deep and rich but subdued, was comforting. He made several calls, the last one to Carlisle and she heard him mention Priscilla's name.

'Is she going to be all right?' she asked when he returned.

'All is well. Priscilla has several broken ribs but none have pierced the lungs. She's as comfortable as can be expected. Would you like to go and see her tomorrow?'

'Yes, please. I hope we'll be friends too.'

'You will, I promise you. She'll want to be a friend. Now you must rest, my love. This has been a heavy day and we both have work tomorrow. Tonight is no time for a celebration but we'll go somewhere special together tomorrow, drink champagne and toast our future.'

Laurie was nearly asleep, exhausted by the evening's events. She lay curled up on the sofa, her cheek against her arm, her eyelashes fluttering on warm moist cheeks. Ben hunted for a cover and found a tartan rug from the back of his car. He tucked it gently about her and when she slid an arm round his neck, he did not pull away.

'Ben,' she whispered. 'Thank you.'

'For what? For being a fool all these weeks? I should have known there was a reason.'

'But when I saw you looking at Priscilla, that afternoon at her cottage, there was something in your face, I couldn't help but think . . .'

'It was envy, humility, and a big dose of wishful thinking. But it wasn't Priscilla I wanted. Even then. It was you.'

He slid close to her side and she shifted slightly, accommodating his long body on the sofa. He let out a sigh as she came into his arms, naturally and unafraid, their bodies fitting and moulding like gloves. But he did no more than touch her with his lips, moving gently over her skin, and stroking her face with his finger tips. They had a long, long way to go before they could make love together as man and woman.

'What about Milly Washbourne, Ben. Will you go and see her?' she murmured against his ear.

'You and your lame ducks. Don't you ever stop thinking about other people? I didn't reckon the independent Miss Washbourne would take too kindly to a visit from an inquisitive professor so I arranged for her to get an invitation to attend a Well Woman Clinic. This is something the group practice in Windermere is trying to make popular.'

'Oh, you are clever,' she sighed happily.

'Miss Washbourne is pretty healthy for her age apparently, except that she is suffering from a mild malnutrition. She spends more on those three cats than she does on herself. She was given some vitamin boosts and eating advice. Buy tinned food for the cats and keep the salmon for her supper.'

'She'll be back to her old ways in a week,' Laurie prophesied.

'Maybe, but she's had a bad fright and she's concerned about what would happen to her cats if she died. So she'll feed herself more sensibly in the future, just for their sakes.'

He outlined the soft curve of her lips, marvelling at their rosy tint, wondering how long he would have to wait before he could crush them with the desire that was burning inside him.

'Will you marry me? I know I must be mad to take on such a handful of wilful woman, but I can't help myself. I shall probably come home every day and find total strangers lying all over the floor while my wife pulls at their necks.'

'Marry you? And you wouldn't mind me carrying on with my Alexander Technique?' Laurie hid her great delight. 'Is this a truce?'

'Yes, I concede that there is something very basically right about your teaching.'

'And you really want to marry me?' She could hardly believe it, her joy was so complete.

'Are you going deaf? Do I have to say everything twice? Perhaps you've got some lake water in your ears. Yes, I want to marry you. We'll find some nice old farmhouse nearer Carlisle to live in and keep the Boathouse on for a weeked cottage. How would you like that?'

'But what about Cumthwaite Hall? You own it.'

'Yes but I don't want to live in it. And surely you wouldn't want me to close the school? No, never fear, the Alexander Technique can thrive and flourish with my blessing. There are far too many hotels around Windermere already. Now, what's your answer? Don't keep me on tenterhooks.'

'I think you ought to think about it . . .'

He exclaimed impatiently, 'Heavens, I've thought of nothing else, since I saw you in your bare feet that first morning, floating round the dining-room at Cumthwaite Hall, admiring the paintings. You looked so elfin, so unreal, like a fairy from the fells. Yet in seconds you were a firecracker, spitting flames and scorching my eyebrows.'

'Darling Ben. Of course, I'll marry you. But I can't change. I can only be the same person.'

'I don't want you to change. I want you to stay exactly the way you are. No more talking, now, my darling. We'll have tomorrow and forever for talking.'

They were the last words that Laurie heard as she closed her eyes, her eyelids heavy with sleep. She was so happy and she knew there was something else she wanted to say to Ben, but her thoughts were already drifting away on a dream that was sweetness itself. His arms closed round her, secure and strong, keeping her safe from the world outside.

The shrill ringing of the telephone woke Laurie from her sleep. She stirred in Ben's arms, amazed to find herself still there at all but moving carefully so that she did not wake him. He was deeply asleep, the stubble on his shadowed chin denoting the passing of the night. She climbed off the sofa, over his legs, and padded quickly over to the telephone.

'Yes, hello,' she said quietly.

'I've some information for Professor Vaughan.'

'He's not available just at the moment.' Laurie looked fondly across at the heap of sleeping manhood sprawled on the sofa. She did not have the heart to wake him. 'Can I take a message?'

'He was asking for the whereabouts of a Nurse Amy Newman, formerly of St Ranulph's. Miss Newman can be located at the Great Ormond Street Hospital for Children where she has been working for the last two years.'

'Great Ormond Street? Then she hasn't left nursing?'

'Not according to our records. She's been nursing consistently apart from one period of leave of absence for health reasons.'

'And she's all right? I mean, she's working and everything?'

There was a silence. 'I have no further information, I'm sorry.'

'Thank you. You've been very kind.'

Laurie went through to the kitchen, filled the electric kettle and switched it on. Amy was nursing again and that must be a good sign. That Saturday night had left its scars on both of them, but at least Amy was still doing the kind of work she loved. And work must be some kind of therapy. Laurie wished she could do something positive to help Amy, but perhaps she ought to stay away. It might be better to remain out of sight, harder but kinder. But at least this knowledge was a start to her own healing.

There was little food in the refrigerator and only enough milk for a cup of tea. But there was plenty of fruit and very quietly she began to make a fruit salad with chopped apples and oranges, nuts and slices of raw pepper. Maybe it was not the kind of breakfast Ben was used to, but it was all she could rustle up.

'You'll be teaching me the semi-supine next,' he growled, opening one eye and taking in the breakfast tray. 'Is this what I can expect for breakfast from now on?''

'What do you usually have?'

'Bacon, fried egg, mushrooms, sausages, fried bread.'

'You're a big fibber. There's nothing remotely like that in your refrigerator. Tell me the truth.'

'Black coffee. I usually eat later.'

'I want to teach you the Alexander Technique, if you'll let me. You do have a slight stoop, right inclined,' she said, feeling shy of him this morning but regarding his strong brown neck with professional eyes.

'Right inclined, eh?' he said, taking a mug of tea, his eyes twinkling. 'Tell me more, I'm fascinated.'

'You probably always go to the righthand side of a patient's bed, and always lean towards him on the right side.'

'Quite the little detective,' he agreed. 'I think I probably do.'

'It's there in your neck. I can see it,' she said. 'Dentists get bad necks, so do cello players. But it's reversible. It's possible to unlearn a habit pattern and find a balanced relationship—'

'Book me a lesson later, teacher,' said Ben amiably. 'Put that mug down and come here. I'm still waiting for my answer. When are you going to tell me? I've got a lecture in two hours and I'm not going to make it if you keep me dangling on a string.'

The carriage clock on his desk began to chime nine. At the small sweet sounds, Laurie jerked back from Ben's arms in dismay. 'And I've got a class! Now! I'm going to be dreadfully late. I've got to get dressed. Where are my clothes . . . oh, heavens . . .' Laurie rushed around, hunting for her track suit.

'It's in the washing machine, waiting to be laundered. Go dressed as you are. Surely someone who has walked through the grounds wearing two bin liners would think nothing of appearing in a modest pair of red pyjamas?'

'You're laughing at me,' she raged at him. 'I can't go back like this, especially at this time in the morning. Everyone will talk. My reputation will be in shreds.

'Let them talk. You spent the night here. It's already in shreds.' They linked hands and began their long slide into an enduring love. 'Tell them you spent the midnight hours with your intended husband. Chastely but in a loving embrace. And then, Laurie darling, when you are ready, perhaps you'll tell me that you love me?'

She gave him one of her big, wide smiles, barely hiding the song in her heart. She was ready now and soon she would give him her answer. But she wanted this one glorious moment to herself and then she would tell him.

LAZE AWAY THE SENSUAL DAYS OF SUMMER . . .

.. WITH SUN, SEA, SAND

AND a special selection of 4 brand new novels in this great Holiday Romance Pack.

You're spoilt for choice with this unique collection which features four popular writers.

EQUAL OPPORTUNITIES — Penny Jordan
ONCE AND FOR ALWAYS — Leigh Michaels
TASMANIAN DEVIL — Valerie Parv
DANGEROUS OBSESSION — Patricia Wilson

The combination of excellent value for money and a pack which will stow away easily on your travels, makes this the hottest summer reading around!

Available from Boots, Martins, John Menzies, W. H. Smith, Woolworths and other paperback stockists.

PUB: 30th JUNE 89   PRICE: £5.00

Doctor Nurse Romances

Romance in modern medical life

Read more about the lives and loves of doctors and nurses in the fascinatingly different backgrounds of contemporary medicine. These are the three Doctor Nurse romances to look out for next month.

INSTANT CARE
Frances Crowne

RESORTING TO MAGIC
Holly North

THE VALLERSAY CURE
Drusilla Douglas

Buy them from your usual paperback stockist, or write to: Mills & Boon Reader Service, P.O. Box 236, Thornton Rd, Croydon, Surrey CR9 3RU, England. Readers in Southern Africa — write to: Independent Book Services Pty, Postbag X3010, Randburg, 2125, S. Africa.

Mills & Boon
the rose of romance

AROUND THE WORLD WORDSEARCH
COMPETITION!

How would you like a years supply of Mills & Boon Romances ABSOLUTELY FREE? Well, you can win them! All you have to do is complete the word puzzle below and send it in to us by October 31st. 1989. The first 5 correct entries picked out of the bag after that date will win **a years supply of Mills & Boon Romances** (*ten books every month - worth around £150*) What could be easier?

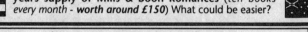

R	D	N	A	L	R	E	Z	T	I	W	S
E	O	N	M	C	H	I	N	A	A	C	C
G	M	U	I	G	L	E	B	N	N	U	O
Y	E	C	E	G	W	H	I	Z	C	B	T
P	D	R	H	S	E	R	I	A	Z	A	L
T	N	S	M	P	E	R	U	N	D	D	A
N	A	W	I	A	T	P	I	I	E	N	N
Y	L	A	T	I	N	A	N	A	N	A	D
N	G	S	T	N	H	Y	D	E	M	L	Q
W	N	O	J	A	M	A	I	C	A	L	A
R	E	L	A	D	A	N	A	C	R	O	R
T	H	A	I	L	A	N	D	D	K	H	I

ITALY	THAILAND	SCOTLAND	SWITZERLAND
GERMANY	IRAQ	JAMAICA	
HOLLAND	ZAIRE	TANZANIA	**PLEASE TURN**
BELGIUM	TAIWAN	PERU	**OVER FOR**
EGYPT	CANADA	SPAIN	**DETAILS**
CHINA	INDIA	DENMARK	**ON HOW**
NIGERIA	ENGLAND	CUBA	**TO ENTER**

HOW TO ENTER

All the words listed overleaf, below the word puzzle, are hidden in the grid. You can find them by reading the letters forward, backwards, up or down, or diagonally. When you find a word, circle it or put a line through it, the remaining letters (which you can read from left to right, from the top of the puzzle through to the bottom) will spell a secret message.

After you have filled in all the words, don't forget to fill in your name and address in the space provided and pop this page in an envelope (you don't need a stamp) and post it today. Hurry - competition ends October 31st. 1989.

Mills & Boon Competition,
FREEPOST,
P.O. Box 236,
Croydon,
Surrey. CR9 9EL
Only one entry per household

Secret Message _____

_____

Name _____

Address _____

_____

_____

_____ Postcode _____

You may be mailed as a result of entering this competition

COMP 6